Unclean Hands 2

By

Aubrey Boyd

This edition was published by Aubrey Boyd. TM are trademarks of the author.

ISBN Paperback: 979-8-9885365-0-5

ISBN eBook: 979-8-9885365-1-2

Printed in the U.S.A.

Dedication

To my ever growing family, both immediate (Dedra, Aubrey J, Diamond, N'diyah, Jontue, Julian and grandchildren) and extended-

I am never afraid to try new things, and neither should you. I will ensure the Boyd Family continues to be respected and I will always try to lead by example.

I love you all

Contents

Acknowledgements

Cover designed by: Tiziana DeRosa

Artwork by: Brandy Antonio www.brandyantonio.com

Edited by: Lynda Tyler, Dedra Boyd and Amber Williams

Prologue

After years of relative peace in the community. A new drug organization comes to town. The once small town of just 100,000 people grew into a mid-size city of over 500,000 people in just 15 years.

Unclean Hands 2 is about two new drug organizations using their political influence and fear tactics to destroy the growing community. Thomas Williams will once again try to expose the truth and stop the spread of drugs.

Chapter 1
The Illicit Rendezvous

Robin Antonio Park is located on the outskirts of town; however, its beautiful landscape makes it immensely popular amongst teenagers for intimate rendezvous. It was quiet, serene, and everything someone would ever need to escape the prying eyes and noise of the streets for a calming and relaxing experience.

In the heart of this tranquil park, a dense grove of lavender and dogwood trees created a picturesque haven of scent and shade. Blades of grass flowed with freedom and even the moonlight from between the trees gave it a calmingly otherworldly vibe. The misty moonlit night illuminated the park in a manner that seemed like it was hiding something.

Under normal circumstances, the park was a serene escape from the hustle and bustle. However, on this moonlit night, it was anything but ordinary of circumstances. It was so far from the center of town that nobody went there as part of their daily routine.

It was a place where the park would be occupied by people performing their morning exercises or daily walks during daytime and the underside of the town would use the location for shady dealings at sun set in its grove. It was a good place for an illegal deal. Especially if there was a need to show force. The lethal kind of force. That is why this place was called 'the cut' as well.

The sound of the car came well before its headlights shone on the bushes, disturbing the peaceful atmosphere. When the car stopped and the doors opened, out came two men of Mexican descent, their faces clearly visible under the park's parking lot lights. It was clear that these men were not here to spend a few hours talking on the benches or walking along the flower trails. They were not here for the lakeside or the rushing water stream. These men were here for shady dealings, and it was a sight when two men stood amidst the lavender, their breath visible in the crisp air as they cast furtive glances around the park. They seemed calm, but in a way that someone would be trying to blend in, even though there was not any crowd to blend into. They were looking around for someone, or something.

As they got out, their weapons (very clearly visible and on display) glinted in the moonlight. They were not hiding the fact that they were well-equipped. They did not need to, not today and not for what was coming. No words were spoken between them because they needed to stay alert, not just for the expected company, but for uninvited guests as well.

Another pair of car headlights emerged in the park and darted towards the two men. In any other circumstance, they would be blinded by the headlights. However, this time they knew exactly where to look. The approaching car's headlights flashed. They could instantly recognize the make and model for the vehicle slowly advancing towards their own; a classic 1969 chevy Camero.

The vehicle came to a stop and the beam of the headlights dimmed until they closed. Two men got out, Black, but that was not what two Mexican men noticed. Rather, the Black that emerged were wearing bullet proof vests to show that they came prepared. However, not in a clever way, for the deal that they had to make that evening. The Mexican men thought "Sure, the Black men would bring some firepower, but bullet proof protection was overkill, something didn't feel right." You did not need bullet proof protection unless you were planning for a robbery. The bullet proof vests the Black men were wearing looked heavy and they were slim men causing them to look awkward.

The Mexicans both went to the back of their car and opened the trunk, bringing out a tote container. It was heavy, quite heavy. One of them could have carried it, but they needed to talk. Something seemed off. Before they walked towards the waiting men it was decided to have a quick conversation amongst themselves.

"¿Protección?" one of them asked, clearly wary of the situation. One of the Mexician men eyed the duffle bags the two Black men were carring on their shoulders while their other hands resting on assault rifles, with the clip protuding out of the holster showcasing some extended clips. The Black men had other protection besides the firearms they had bought with them.

"¿Cómo les va, caballeros esta noche?" One of the two Black men said. He must have been the leader of the two.

The Mexican man's partner responded as they bought the tote container forward. "No sabíamos qué hablas Español amigo." He kept his gun close but relaxed a bit. He kept one finger on his gun's trigger just in case, with perfect discipline, ready to open fire. "De donde eres?" He asked, as he moved near a rock and some bushes, large enough that if he ducked behind it the two Black men would not be able to see him—or shoot at him, for that matter.

"You Dominican or something? If not, I guess we will need to be cautious of what words that come out our mouths moving forward." He put his foot on one of the smaller rocks as he did. "Dale'!" He looked at his partner, who pushed the tote container forward, carefully.

The leader of the two Black men stepped forward, asserting himself, but making sure to seem more relaxed as he dropped the duffle bag and moved towards them. "Gentlemen, I assure you that is as far as my Spanish aspiration goes. I do not know shit else."

The men began to laugh and the tense atmosphere; though short lived, calmed down a bit. None of them were trusting each other just yet. All had bought some very visible, exceptionally large guns and it was not just the fact that any could open fire at any minute. It was the idea of someone else hiding in the bushes, or even of police officers entering the park and arresting them. Even if none of them could pin them to the drugs, they were still carrying weapons that was not registered. That could lead to a prison sentence.

The leader of the Black men smiled, his shoulders dropping as he put down his guard. "All joking aside, did you bring the product?" he asked. He could see the tote container, but he still wanted to ask that question. It was necessary to get things done right. He knew the Mexicans were sticklers for protocol and he did not want to show the others that something was afoot.

One of the Mexican men laughed. "Of course, of course!" he exclaimed; his arms outstretched as he pointed towards his partner. The man was tall and has a bulky frame. He hovered above the plastic-looking container. "But" he added, "…can you show us the money first? We know how you people like to play games and not have all the money." He could see the other man out the corner of his eye, his fingers were twitching as he said it. "I'm just saying." the Mexican man added further, raising his hands.

The two men were clearly vexed, and his comment did not do anything to address it or make it better. "What the fuck do you mean "you people"?" the leader asked. The Black other had not spoken anything just yet, and that was something that the Mexican man noted. "This is not how I envisioned this transaction would go this evening. I am blown right now."

The second Black man finally spoke as he began to walk forward. "You guys are supposed to be our new suppliers and you insult us. That is fucked up." He stopped by his partner and asked him for his duffle bag. He winked at him too, but the Mexican man did not notice that. He even missed the clear, very visible smile on the leader of the two as he handed his slimmer companion the bag.

The second Black man then walked with the duffle bag towards the Mexicans. He was not smiling. He quickly hands the Mexican the bag and smiles back. The other slim Black man walks towards the Mexicans with a serious look on his face. He dropped the duffle bag and opened it up, showing stacks on stacks of US dollars.

But it was the leader of the Black men that spoke up. "As you can see, we have your money. Now it is your turn. Where is the fucking product?"

The Mexican man looked at the duffle bag, then at his partner and nodded. The other Mexican man began to bring the tote container towards them. He looked back towards the duffle bag and then at the leader of the two Black men and smiled.

"I like this Negrito," he said, pointing towards the duffle bag and the money. "Sure, we have the product. Hell, we never leave home without it. What 'chu saying!" His hand reached towards his companion as he walked next to him carrying the container.

The other Mexican man pointed towards the container and instructed him to open the large plastic lid. "Abre lo ese!" he said, as he saw the leader of the Black men and his slimmer partner walk towards them. They were quite close now and the Mexican man was very aware that he had given up his cover. The Mexicans who were also wearing bullet proof vests under their clothing positioned himself close to a large boulder just in case he needed cover of gunfire. However, if someone opened fire, he would have a few seconds to take cover. It was a fool's errand, but it was better to have something than nothing.

As the plastic lid opened, they could all see the tightly packed container with all its square blocks of off-white substances. Their plastic wraps had tape around them, and it was clear what it was from the look of the inner product to the wrapping around it. The Black leader's companion walked towards the container, his eyes having a questioning look towards the Mexican men. They both nodded, and at the same time, he pulled out a testing kit. Even amateurs evaluated all their bricks and despite their show of force, it was clear that they at least knew what they were doing.

He first inspected one of the bricks up close from the outside before looking towards his partner and giving the thumbs up. Then, as his companion was evaluating the product, the leader added, "Yes, it looks good from here, but I need to evaluate it first. We know how you people like to play games and not sell the right stuff. Need to make sure it is not baking soda under there."

No sooner were those words spoken that the façade of niceties came down and the smiling faces of the Mexican men were replaced with one of scorn.

"You made your point 'ese. Now quickly, hurry up and do what you need to do to evaluate the product. Dale'!" The Mexican man and his partner were getting uneasy. The Black men had come with vests and insulted them to their faces more than once. Even when criminals interacted, there was a certain etiquette expected. Clearly these two Black men were trying to stoke the fire and then pour gasoline onto it.

The slimmer Black man pierced one of the square blocks and placed some of the powder substance in a tube of solution. He held the tube upright and squeezed it. Next, the man began to shake the tube for about ten seconds and the color of the liquid changed to a turquoise color. This confirmed that the substance was cocaine. The Mexican men knew that it would, but he still felt relieved. That relief was short lived as the man reached in the container once again for another bag.

"What are you doing?" he asked him. "Just checking" the slim Black man replied. His response came quick too. The slim Black man repeated the same procedure; he pierced it with a blade and checked the substance in a small container. Once again, this one turned turquoise as well.

The slimmer man once again gave a thumbs up to his partner and gave him another winked, yet again missed by his Mexican adversaries. "Yo, we good over here! Give these motherfuckers the money."

Satisfied with the outcome, the leader walked over with the other duffle bag and put it beside his partner. Both Black men carried one of each.

The leader of the two Black men was still smiling as he handed the money over. He looked over to his partner and he smiled back. The Mexican man put the lid on the container and pushed it towards the other two men. Then they both began counting the money.

The Black men, though, did not touch the product just yet. The Mexican men would have noticed it if both were not distracted. Usually in moments like these, there was a lot less agitation and a lot less threat from weapons. The relief that both Mexican men got had them thinking that the deal was over.

Once they were distracted with counting the money, the slim Black man shot the closet Mexican man in the back of the head. His partner grabbed his weapon and started firing in their direction. The lead Mexican man sprinted for cover, taking position behind the large boulder. The Mexican man managed to retreat with the money and some drugs, but he did not get too far before the two Black men flanked beside him and began shooting. Bullet after bullet was unloaded and the Mexican man quickly fell to the ground and died from multiple gunshot wounds.

The moonlit night had become a bloodbath, even though it unfolded quickly. The ground was caked in blood, and it was very visible under the moonlight, red and dark as blood can be.

The two Black men quickly gathered up the duffle bags. The slimmer one carried them both to the car while the leader of the two took the tote container and hurried it to the trunk of their Chevy Camero.

However, in their haste, they did not see the two bricks of cocaine they had taken out for testing had fallen on the ground since both parties had turned their headlights off for the ordeal. Attracting unnecessary attention was not needed and the moonlit night and parking lot lights were enough. The bricks of cocaine were left behind as the larger container was secured safely in the trunk. The two Black men sped away from location using another exit out of Robin Antonio Park.

Chapter 2
Unveiling Shadows

The moon had now retreated beyond the horizon, leaving the sky free for the brilliant sun to take center stage. The warm and radiant light bathed Robin Antonio Park in a golden glow, awakening the world from its nocturnal slumber. As the sun's first rays pierced the morning mist, they danced playfully above the gentle stream, casting shimmering reflections upon its tranquil surface.

Under the sun's gaze, the park transformed into a tapestry of vibrant colors and textures. The grass now glistened with dewdrops that sparkled like a myriad of tiny diamonds. Trees, stretching their branches toward the heavens, seemed to reach for the sun's nourishing embrace.

Birds chirped melodious songs from the treetops, celebrating the arrival of a new day. Their tunes harmonized with the rustling leaves, creating a symphony of nature's awakening. Squirrels and rabbits, emboldened by the daylight, ventured out from their burrows, scurrying about the park in search of their morning sustenance. The vibrant blooms of wildflowers and the delicate petals of roses unfurled, displaying their intricate beauty for all to admire.

It was everything that this park was famed for amongst the locals. Everything that this serene atmosphere brought laid bare on the surface. But in that unveiling, everything that the night had concealed was now clear. It was a new day, a fresh canvas upon which life's stories would continue to unfold under the benevolent guidance of the sun's radiant presence. There was a story already unfolding here, but that scene was soon disturbed with red, white, and blue.

Only hours after the massacre occurred at the park, the police were at the crime scene. The winter sun formed a mist of its own, the air was more still today. It was like it was giving way for the people moving around the crime scene to conduct their business without being disturbed by nature. It was as if the park was giving way to them, inviting them to something sinister.

Yellow tape was installed, and white caulk drawn around the two bodies, the car and around the two bricks of cocaine. It was clear at first sight that this was not some random shootout, but was it a deal gone wrong? Was it a taste of things to come, or would this be it? It was evident that some illegal dealings did not go so well for the two Mexican men found dead at the scene with multiple close range bullet wounds. One of them had parts of his head missing, the back of the head, to be precise.

Detective Kelly noted every single detail he could as he started his investigation. He had a notepad, and he made some notes on one page. Turned it around and wrote a bit of something else on another. He did this all the while standing next to his car, not yet approaching the crime scene closely. It was clear that this man was the leading police officer at the crime scene with the air of importance he carried around himself, but to what extent? His attitude told another story because it was not often that you found a detective on scene eating beef jerky as he viewed two bodies gruesomely murdered.

"So, what happened here?" he asked one of the police officers on the scene. "Goddamn, I forgot that the city even had a park this far out from downtown." He began to say to the officer. Said the officer had just started to explain the situation but paused for the detective. After that he began to ramble. "This place is nice! Far… but not too far, you know! Isolated, but nice!"

The detective looked around, and the officer on scene continued to wait patiently. Any other junior police officer and any other detective; this exchange would have gone on very differently. However, Detective Kelly did have a reputation of being slightly unorthodox, though that was putting it mildly.

"I need to look at the city map again." He spoke. "I just might have to come back and check this place out."

The officer waited a bit and both him and the detective began looking at each other. "Um…yeah," he started, stammering a bit, "Yeah Detective, this is nice. An isolated place indeed." He lifted his hand to point towards the ground. "Look at this." He pointed to two bricks of cocaine on the ground, bits of powder scattered around the area. "One of the police officers found this package on the ground. We are going to seal it as evidence."

Detective Kelly had taken another bite of his beef jerky, but as soon as the police officer pointed him towards the two packages on the ground, he spit it out, unchewed. "Hold up. Let me see that package first." He began walking towards where the officer had pointed.

The detective reached into his pocket and quickly put on a pair of rubber gloves. He adjusted his pants as he crouched on the ground, examining the packages. "Could I have something to pick up the evidence with?" he asked the police officer, still looking towards the package, beginning to hold out his hand. The officer handed him a large pair of tongs and he looked at one of the packages.

Detective Kelly lifted the brick, very clearly noticing the piercing and the powder. What occurred was clear, but the 'why' of it all was the big question. As he lifted the brick of cocaine, he turned it around and noticed a red chili pepper stamped on the package. It was not too red, but it was bright enough that it would be hard to miss. Detective Kelly looked up at the police officer, who had just as much of a shocked look on his face as the detective. The police officer produced an evidence bag, and the detective carefully placed it in. He then examined the second brick of cocaine as well. It was the same marking. Red Chili Pepper. The detective placed the second bag in evidence as well.

"What the heck is that?" Detective Kelly exclaimed, questioningly; clearly not expecting the police officer to answer. "I have not seen this marking on any other drugs we've confiscated before." He looked at the two bricks of cocaine in the evidence bag and pointed his finger towards them. "This is new to me. Could this mean we have a new drug supplier in town?" He stared in the direction of the police officer, thinking as the officer began to move forward to take the package from him.

"Oh, yes. "Replied the officer. Detective Kelly handed the evidence bag to the officer. "Put this in with the rest, we are going to have CSI and the drug task force look at this later. Make sure you do not miss any of that powder in the ground."

The police officer went and deposited the evidence, coming back towards Detective Kelly as he called the rest of the officers in and got as much information as he could from them. The lead police officer gave them each something to do and instructed them as he needed. The two Mexican men that lay dead on the ground were nowhere near as important as the marking on the package. The two Mexican men were deadbeats, pushers, drug users, abusers, small time gangsters; whatever one wants to call them. However, the one they were working for would be the point of interest.

It was not long before the local media started swarming the scene and Detective Kelly could already see a few police officers preventing them from entering, though there was one that Kelly could never have missed. In a crowd of reporters, he noticed one journalist in particular, Thomas Williams.

Thomas Williams' grandfather was an old employer of Detective Kelly's. Now a veteran reporter for the Southern Times, it was unusual for him to be at a crime scene these days. He had already made his mark in his career, and a man like that was more often found sipping drinks at the bar or having the time of his life on a golf course rather than up and about this early. Thomas was a person of action, yes, but he had seen action, and had done too much in too short a time to rest on his laurels.

He was the reason Robin Antonio Park could exist after all. Not because he had a hand in its creation but rather because the town could now experience a semblance of peace and calm. He had been a major player in bringing down the town's crime rate and it was clear that the tables were turning again. The once small town with a population of just 100,000 had now grown into something else, a proper city, even. Growing five-times with more than half a million residents in just fifteen years was a huge feat of its own. That kind of rapid growth was always sure to bring some shady people and unwanted activity.

Robin Antonio Park though, was a testament of that effort. The community was able to see this serene place, away from the noise and uproar. Unfortunately, the peace had now disturbed; it was truly a sign of the times. Robin Antonio Park was rarely used by the town's citizens as it was, and even fewer would come here now, fearing falling victim to crime, or to the criminals.

Detective Kelly tried to ignore his calls for answers by the press, but Thomas Williams' voice rang clearer and louder than the rest. The man was persistent, he gave him that. Detective Kelly knew he could not walk away without at least entertaining him a bit first.

When Thomas Williams got past the crime scene line, it was clear there was no stopping him. The detective braced for a talk, one he knew was going to boil his blood, if not put him in a fit of rage. "Kelly, what happened here? Was this crime related to drugs?" Thomas began asking; his recorder already on and ready to capture every word. "It is rare to have any crime this far away from the inner city. Do you care to elaborate on the two dead bodies?"

"First, it's Detective Kelly, Thomas" the detective replied, sternly. He did not know if he had interrupted the reporter, or he had finished speaking. Kelly usually walks over about anyone else, but not Thomas Williams. As much as Detective Kelly liked to play the bully role with other police officers, the detective knew how to play the game of kindness in front of others; and the Thomas knew that he did, too.

"Second, there will be no statement at this time. Also just think Thomas, if your grandfather were still around this little calamity would have made him a pretty penny would you not agree?" That last bit was a bit more accusatory than the rest, but that was the detective's intention. There was nothing more satisfying than to hang dark clouds over other people's heads and watch them crumble.

Thomas Williams looked irked by Detective Kelly's words; but he stood firm, and swiftly replied. "He would have made money from these men's burials, yeah." He began, but the detective began walking away from him at a faster pace.

Thomas had to keep up with him as he continued. "But we would still need someone to escort the bodies to the cemetery, wouldn't we? Someone to keep an eye on things?" His voice was as quick and stale as ever, but his eyes did all the talking the detective needed to see. Even though he was looking ahead as he walked, he could still feel the reporter gauging him. "Are you still up for the job officer?" The reporter paused as soon as he said the words, quickly swallowing and speaking again, "I mean, Detective Kelly?"

"Well, I am sure you could not afford me anymore. Plus, since the Williams funeral home is no more, it looks like I will be work for the new nigger funeral home everyone is raving about" the detective answered. There was a sharpness to his tone that cut through the conversation. "I hear that they do an excellent job and don't move drugs with the dead bodies either."

"Is that so?" Thomas replied, unfazed by the man's demeanor. The detective would have riled anyone else up, but he knew the kind of words these men spoke to spark one's ire, hoping for them to break. "Though, come to think of it, shouldn't your main concern be solving these men's murders, detective?" Thomas laid the question bare. He knew how to hit back, and he did it with his head held high. "Or is it again unsolvable due to their skin color?" Thomas pressed again. "I have heard that only crimes related to white people get solved these days from your department, detective." It was a moment that clearly influenced the detective. Detective Kelly slowed his walking pace for a moment but regained composure and continued walking at pace. "Does your department only wash a certain kind of dirty laundry, Detective Kelly?"

"Well, you and your kind have nothing to worry about, Thomas." The detective answered quickly. He was not in a hurry, but he was not about to let the reporter get the best of him, either. "Now stay your ass behind that yellow tape, boy!" He pointed to where he had first seen Thomas Williams initially. He did not wait to see the reporter return to his original location before the harassing questions.

Detective Kelly himself walked slowly away from Thomas Williams but he did not want to appear that he was in a hurry. Kelly thought the reporter was too smart for his own good, but it was clear he did not want someone with a mic and a recording device within fifty feet of the crime scene, least of all in situations like this.

Robin Antonio Park had plenty of places to hide. Not wanting to take a risk, the detective chose a secluded but still noisy area near a stream. When he determined that he was well hidden, he took out his phone and made a call.

As the phone rang, he began to wonder what would happen now that a new problem had emerged. Reporter Thomas Williams was just a fly he needed to swat away, but someone else was clearly trying to become a major player in the drug game; and the detective needed to find out how to either extort him or arrest him.

The phone was picked up after the third ring, but nobody answered. To the detective, it was the green light.

"I am sorry to disturb you, especially at this hour, but we may have a problem." He spoke quietly enough that nobody nearby could hear but loud enough that the water stream would not outright make him inaudible. "There is a problem at home, you know. Raccoons, or squirrels. You never know."

The conversation would not make too much sense, but it did not need to, at least not to any third parties that might be listening. "I cannot get into all the details yet, though there seems to be new marks on the furniture I did not recognize. I think we would need to find out who is marking up our furniture."

Then the phone line was cut off, and that was that.

Chapter 3
Sinister Alliance

Lisa Chin was a woman who often interacted with others but did not really confine much with those she met. Her business was one where discretion would always be the better choice, though mistakes were often made. She and her son, Ricky Chin-Davis (or 'Little Ricky,' as everyone called him), lived in a modest size home on the edge of town.

Lisa and Little Ricky were forced to move to the outskirts of town after a family disagreement. Of course, 'family disagreement' was put mildly; but that is what parents did for their children. It had been 15 years since the murder of Little Ricky's father, and Lisa Chin was desperately trying to raise her son away from street violence and corruption, something she was familiar with, especially in her line of work.

Breakfast that morning was the usual. Cereal with milk, but no sugar. Little Ricky liked having sugar, but his mother insisted on not eating it. She wanted him to stay healthy at his age and he always wanted to be a good son to his mother. Though that did not stop him from sneaking a couple scoops of sugar into his milk. It should be said, though, that Little Ricky, despite the name, was not too young either. The boy had grown plenty, even though the name had stuck. His mother still treated him like a child at times, but Little Ricky did not mind.

The mother and son were having breakfast at the kitchen table and the television was on. The television was an older model even though they could afford a new TV. However, it was a memory of times past that Lisa Chin preferred to keep. It got the job done as they did not need to waste money on flashy things. Buying expensive stuff puts you in some unwanted crosshairs too.

Breakfast was usually a silent affair, and the TV was the only sound that was heard in the Chin's home, or at least, conversation was not sparked until necessary. Whatever they were watching halted for the commercial break and the first thing that came was a familiar name and tune.

This is Richard Kelly's Ford and Nissan Auto shop, where your job is your credit. Remember, here there is no credit check and with as little as a deposit of $99 down, you can drive away with a brand-new Ford or Nissan of your choice!

The sound of chewing and the clinking of the spoons stopped as drew their attention to the commercial.

At Rickard Kelly's Ford and Nissan, do like our mascot Kelly the frog and jump over here for these great deals! Why have a boat when you can helm a yacht?

It was Little Ricky who spoke first. "Damn, Richard Kelly is giving cars away. My crew and I are going to get us some new wheels soon" he said with a bunch of cereal still in his mouth. His mother lightly struck him on his shoulder.

"Little Ricky shut your ass up!" She exclaimed. "You know your half black ass is not going to be caught dead driving a damn Ford or Nissan" she goaded him. "All you know is BMW and Mercedes Benz, with that hundred-thousand-dollar shine and coat, with your spoiled ass. You are not fooling anybody!" Lisa laughed.

Little Ricky raised an eyebrow as his head turned towards his mother. "That is true" he said, a smirk visible on his face. "Who was it that spoiled me anyway, ma?"

"Oh, that was me!" his mother shot back, still laughing. "I did that all by myself too." A bit of cereal and milk escaped from her mouth as she said it and she had to catch it with her spoon.

"Anyway, did you hear about what happened at the park? You know, at Robin Antonio Park? The one just a few miles from here?" She took a bite of her cereal as she looked to her son, examining his reaction. He seemed uninterested.

"I do not want you or your fucked up crew spending time together there, you hear?" she said, a bit louder, quite sternly, too. "Shit is getting crazy. I would have never gotten a place anywhere near that park if I knew it would be that bad of a place." She began to speak to herself more than her son, who listened quietly. He knew that he had to let her speak or he would get a smack on his noggin.

"Hell, who knew that it would end up becoming a murder crime scene one day. What was the fucking point of moving us out this damn far in bumfuck nowhere to still deal with the same shit again? I lost your father to that shit, you hear, and I am not losing my baby the same way. Do you understand Little Ricky?" She began to caress his hair as she spoke.

"Yes ma." he said, cringing a bit at his mother's touch, but knowing better than to even try to swat her hand away. "I am not a kid anymore, though." I am 19 years old now, and I got this. I can take care of myself."

"I know baby" his mother responded, clearly not willing to let go of the matter.

"Nothing is going to happen to us, ma. I am ready to start contributing to the bills around here, too. You know I am the co-head of the household now. I am a full grow ass man!" He propped his chin up and stiffened his shoulders, as if to assert himself. He sat up in his chair, rearranging his posture to one where he could be seen as important.

"Boy, sit your ass down" his mother responded kindly, clearly thinking of his antics as nothing. "You just worry about finishing college. I got everything else. Our family needs a lawyer. Someone that will not charge us for legal advice, Pro bono stuff. It is easy to get a good one for that. You know this family is always in some shit."

They resumed eating their breakfast; Neither were paying attention at this point. "Now, I must take care of some business today. Make sure this house 'doors are locked, and the burglar alarm is turned on when you leave. Here is $200 dollars for food and whatever else you want, baby." She handed her son the money, but he was busy with his breakfast, so she put the money on the table, under a saltshaker.

"Mommy might not come home tonight if she is lucky, all right babies? I am trying to get under someone if you what I mean?" She looked at him, though her son's response was one that she did not like. She wanted to be able to talk to him about things like this, even if it made him uncomfortable. To whom else would she talk? She needed him to understand that he should never get into this kind of life.

"I do not want to hear that shit mom!" he had said, quickly. "Whatever you do is your business just let the guy know I am not calling him Dad." He put down his spoon. "Plus, like I always tell you, I do not need any money. I still have a few stacks left over from yesterday. Now, enjoy yourself. I love you, Mom! Behave yourself!"

"I love you more baby," she said as she kissed his forehead, hurrying to leave the house. "And I'll tell you something, do not have your little dirty ass friends in my living room." She pointed one finger towards him, as a warning. "You know the rules."

"I know the living room is for show only and your company, ma," he said, as if the line was rehearsed. He had said it a thousand times already during the days that his mom left. "I got it mom."

Lisa Chin left the house with an overnight bag and some confidence. She knew her son was up to no good, but she was trying her best to make sure he at least gets the idea of second guessing himself before he makes some stupid decisions. Once she drove down the street and turned the corner, Little Ricky saw her leave through the window. He quickly reached for his phone and sent a few text messages. After that, he made a call.

"Yo, I need you all to meet me at my house in 30 minutes. We got to cut this stuff today. I will have the house to myself tonight, so bring all the products and money,"

he quickly said. On the phone, he could have been more careful; he should have. Since in his hurry, things were forgotten, and carelessness gave way to recklessness.

"I want to get rid of all the products in one week, all right? We are not pushers, guys. We are not some small-time, big-time dealers. Shit, we rob them. Let us be real, who are they going to tell? The police? Those police officers cannot do shit! How are they going to help them? It is perfect. Now hurry up!"

If they had been drug dealers, they would have realized to be less…open about their extracurricular activities, but Little Ricky was not exactly born subtle.

*****

Meanwhile, Detective Kelly was visiting the Richard Kelly Ford and Nissan dealership to talk to the owner himself. Some might say their names were the only things they had in common, but the detective would have said that power and ambition were the two things always inherent; never acquired, and that those were their most common traits.

But that was also why the detective did not like it when he was instructed to wait in the lobby until Mr. Kelly was available. *People should be available for me, not the other way around,* he thought to himself. He knew that in his world, respect had to be earned the hard way and he was nothing if not the kind to bear a few scratches as he took what he wanted.

Richard Kelly was the owner of the car dealership, but that is not all that he was. As it turns out, selling repossessed vehicles as new and running one of the largest crime rings and drug organizations in town were professions that perfectly synergized (each profited) from their association.

Just like his dealership, his organization logo itself is the leaping frog. An outsider familiar with both would have made the connection in an instant, which is exactly why Richard Kelly knew it was the perfect cover. "Right under your nose!" He would say to the detective, at times, as he had asked on more than one occasion why the man took the same mantle of his drug organization as perfectly legitimate one.

Of course, Richard knew how to play the game, too. He often used his power and influence to control the local politicians and the police department. He could hold up detectives until he was ready to entertain them, as he was just now. It took a while, but after a few minutes Richard Kelly emerged from his office.

"What a pleasure to see you Detective Kelly! How can I help you today? Did the police department enjoy the new Ford Crown Victoria squad cars I donated?"

The man was a businessperson at heart, the detective noted. Direct and efficient, not missing a beat, something that was used often against people that preferred to skirt around the truth.

"Yes sir, everyone is happy; and they all give thanks to you again for your generosity. Your donations are much appreciated," said the detective. Of course, nothing was free, and the detective knew that. The man would hold this over the police department, as did any other politician who bought his colleagues through donations.

"Anything to help the police officers, eh, detective? Cause at Richard Kelly Ford and Nissan blue lives matter too!" The man's enthusiasm was no façade, and that was why the detective referred to him as 'sir.'

"Good to hear that. May we talk in your office, sir?"

"Sure!" He exclaimed, before he waved to get the attention of the woman sitting outside his office door. "Alcia, please let everyone know that I am in a meeting. Hold my calls."

"Sure, Richard." The woman replied, getting up from her chair but not moving further. She was not expecting Richard to stop, either. "However, I need to talk to you later about some accounting issues."

"Alright, all right, Alcia. After my meeting with the detective," he replied as she slowly sat back down. Alcia Adams was the head accountant at Richard Kelly's dealership. She always had a knack for numbers and kept accounts for every penny spent at the dealership, though of course that job came with some additional, unofficial responsibilities.

The detective did not waste any time as they reached the office. "Richard, we have a problem," he said as he closed the door behind him. "We found a couple of murdered Mexicans on the outskirts of town at Robin Antonio Park."

"Okay, some dead Mexicans. What is the damn problem?" Richard Kelly responded, uninterested in the event, or at least, so far.

"It is not the Mexicans that are the problem; we found a kilo of cocaine and it was not one of yours." The detective saw the man's eyes dart towards his own. It was surreal, seeing this old geezer seemed scary. "The package had a red chili pepper logo stamped on it. So, either you changed logos or there is a new drug organization in town."

There was silence for a while, and Richard took his chin in his hands as he thought for a good minute. "Well, it damn sure is not mine. We only use the leaping green frog over here baby!" His tone changed back to his enthusiastic self, and the detective was very wary of this. The man was after a challenge, and he had found it. "Now what are you going to do about this problem, detective?"

Damn. The detective thought to himself. He is already cashing in.

"Those new cars are not free damnit. What were they? Ford Crown Victorias if I am not mistaken, correct?" He asked the detective. "The deal is I will supply you all with cars and other things. You in return make sure I am the only supplier of drugs in this city. Now, do we have a misunderstanding? Or do you understand?"

The jolly tone was back, but the words did not match the tone.

"Absolutely, I just thought you wanted to be aware of this new threat," the detective replied, far quicker than he would have wanted. He knew it did not matter, but he did not want to show his vulnerability in front of the man.

"No, no, you were right to inform me, and I apologize for being harsh," Richard responded. His words were genuine, but the truly clear threat was still there. "I just got a lot of pressure on me, and I cannot afford more competition."

Suddenly, there was a knock on the door. Alcia Adams peaked through, reminding Richard Kelly about an urgent matter.

"I am so sorry to bother you gentlemen," she said as she came in. "Although, I must talk to Mr. Kelly in private Now!"

The detective could not be happier at the interruption, but he kept his cool.

"Detective Kelly would you please excuse us and thank you again for stopping by. Go checkout the new Ford Mustang while you are here. Hell, son, take it for a test drive!"

"No thank you," replied to the detective. I must get back to work. You all have a wonderful day." The detective briskly walked towards the exit. He walked out of the office and Alcia immediately told Richard Kelly her concerns. The detective was still within earshot, but he did not make out everything she said, only bits and pieces.

"Richard, we have a major problem," she told her boss.

"Are you kidding me, asked Richard. Is that all anyone can say to me today? Not, 'Hi Richard I love the new TV ad' or 'Richard you look amazing in your new suit today'?

There was no pause before she answered. "Richard, you look amazing in your new suit."

"Why thank you! It is Italian, you know. Real stuff. Now, what is so damn important this time?" he asked.

The woman cleared her throat and regained her composure a bit. The comment had clearly thrown her off. "We are making too much money at the dealership and the car sales are not reflecting the increase in profits."

"Hello? That is great news," the old man answered, bewildered at the suggestion that it was not. "Show me the profits!"

Alcia sighed. She knew she was dealing with a difficult man, but even this was not something that took too much thinking to understand. She knew he understood it very well, which is where her frustrations truly lay.

"No, it is not a good thing. The IRS has already audited us twice in the last two years. Eventually, they will find something. I cannot keep editing the books. We need to make some changes soon."

"Let me worry about the profits," he cut her off. "I will donate some funds to some Black church or youth center. That always took care of the problem in the past. Just do your part and I will do mine, okay."

"Look Richard, I love you like family, but I am not going to prison over no stupid shit. Please take care of this shit as soon as possible. Use some of that Richard Kelly magic."

The man, for all his power, had a soft spot for some people. He could have squeezed where it hurt, but power is not power if not executed effectively. He let it go, for now, and smiled.

"Do not worry. There is always some Richard Kelly magic darling. Besides, we are like family here and families take care of each other. Now, forget about this silly issue and enjoy your day."

Alcia knew that she had crossed a line. She knew he had asked her something impossible, but that is what the people in power did. They asked others to do the impossible and they took the credit—unless they needed someone else to do it for them.

Chapter 4
Surprising Twist

Thomas Williams briskly walked across the open floor offices of the News Station 7 in the afternoon with a few documents and files in his hand. He quickly made his way past the many monitor screens displaying the latest incidents and events happening locally. Thomas, in all his years, had never really paid attention to too much of his overall surroundings. He was an extremely focused man. If he was not looking directly at something, he might as well not be looking at anything at all.

Today, he was filling in for one of his colleagues at work. A news anchor, who would typically never miss a day of work, was ill. Therefore, Thomas filled his position and being that he was quite the superstar in the community of reporters and journalists in that area. It was natural that he visited News Station 7 often as a guest anchor.

Thomas Williams also had a reputation of being fair, honest, and was very well-liked by some of the locals and many of his peers. However, he was relentless when it came to getting a story. This quite often caused Thomas to make plenty of enemies too. These enemies were at times very wary of the reporter.

At the news station, Thomas did not need to be told what to do. All he needed was someone to hand him a few notes and he was ready to begin the newscast. Thomas quickly glances over the news notes provided before the cameras start rolling. Once the news producer shouted, we are taping. Thomas was surprised by what he read. Camera #1 caught the very visible shock on his face as he took a moment to gather himself before he began reciting from the teleprompter.

"This news is just in. Two teens have died of prescription drug overdose on two consecutive days this week."

He thought of what this could mean; a new drug breaking into the city, he continued,

"Both were from the upscale Hampton Heights area of our city. The drugs Oxycodone and Percocet were found in both teens' systems and are verified as their cause of deaths."

The drugs had already reached one of the poshest neighborhoods of the city; the kind of place where the residents were too wealthy to turn to anything other than white collar crime. This city did not let anyone keep their hands clean, though in this place, clean hands were not even the exception. They just did not exist. Those that got here did so with Unclean Hands too, and those that had been here were still resting on the laurels of their parents and grandparents.

"This is becoming a new trend in our community. This Generation Z enjoys legally approved prescribed medications over the traditional street drugs like marijuana, cocaine, and heroin," read Thomas.

"Leave it to them to make sure even the drugs they take are of a different class and variety." More news after this short commercial break."

The TV producer yelled Break, thereby giving the reporters a few minutes to relax. Thomas was contemplating the turn of events as soon as the shout was heard. Hence, it took a good minute before he heard the local meteorologist ask him a question about the overdose story.

"Thomas, did I hear you right? A few teenagers OD'd in the Heights? Isn't that where all the preppies come from?"

Hampton Heights was more than just the upper-class side of town. The neighborhood was private, closed off. No one could gain access inside this gated community unless approved by the Homeowner Association.

"You heard me correctly." Thomas replied. "I am just as shocked as you. It is a chilly day in hell when you miss the days when the kids sought a few hits of weed for a few bucks from the corner shop. They did not know much better back then. Oxycodone and Percocet are the new drugs of choice for these New Age kids it seems. It is a different kind of high these kids are looking for these days."

Thomas was right. Whether the parents got rich through legal means or otherwise, there was always the likelihood that the rich kids would know exactly where to get new trending drugs. Just because Hampton Heights was an upper-class area did not mean it was immune to this opioid epidemic.

"Well, you know, I have heard stories for a while now. The parents themselves smoke more pot than their children ever will," replied the Meteorologist. The two men nodded to each other in agreement as the Meteorologist continued the conversation. "I bet the police have their hands full with the prescription shit. The parents are rich enough to get the best drugs on the market, legal or otherwise."

"What do you think Thomas?" asked the Meteorologist.

"Absolutely, you are right. I mean, who knows, I might have to put on my investigation hat and find the underlying cause of this story," replied Thomas.

However, he knew that dealing with street crime was quite different than dealing with crime within rich families and their neighborhoods. While the former threatened you and your family, the latter kept you alive and buried you in debt, by false accusations, or legal fees—just to name a few ways.

Just then the producer's voice was heard, "Ten seconds before we are back to life, people. Places everyone!"

Thomas, along with the rest of the news crew quickly got back to their positions. They were ready for a long day of questions from the community on the myriad of stories being uncovered about rising crime in the city.

*****

Detective Kelly was being intensely briefed by his superiors about the overdosed teens' deaths. The detective knew he had to be extremely focused on this case and was determined to find the drugs suppliers, for more than one reason. It was a part of his job but there were far more things riding on in this case. He did not want Richard Kelly to assume that he could not take care of business and allow more drugs competition within the city to diminish his profits. Detective Kelly knew that Richard Kelly was the kind of person that simply did not hold grudges against people then, because he took matters into his own hands or orders. Richard would kill you and your family just to make a point. Therefore, having Richard Kelly as a potential adversarial force was a tough situation. Even Detective Kelly did not want the dealership owner for an enemy of his.

Detective Kelly's sergeant explained to him all the latest findings in both overdose cases and the detective noted everything on in his pad. "As you know, Detective Kelly, both teens are from Hampton Heights. I know you live in that community too, so, I want you to take the lead in this case. The Police Chief and I are aware of your…let us say…commitment to keep that part of the city drug free and we commend you for that," replied the sergeant with a sly grin on his face as he briefed the detective.

However, the sergeant's voice tone turned serious soon after the cunning grin. "Listen, Kelly…" he began. It was not often that the sergeant called him only by his last name, so he knew he was being genuine. "We both live on that side of town. The Police Chief and I prefer to live in a community where our children are safe. Just because we work in these crime-ridden streets does not mean we want to live there too. So, just…do whatever you need to do to solve these crimes, all right," said the sergeant.

“Believe me, I’m on it, sergeant,” confirmed Detective Kelly. “Every low life in town knows better than to sell or do anything illegal on that side of the city. If they do, they know I will be personally overseeing their case. So, give me free reign to investigate this one as I see fit and I will bring in suspect soon, or at least, soon enough.”

“No worries, Detective Kelly. You will have all the resources you need,” uttered the sergeant. “Just remember, that we are dealing with prescription drugs here. In the end you will have to inform me of how high you want this to go. We do not want big pharmaceutical companies coming for us, too. They got some deep pockets and I do not think anybody that lives here could ever manage to rattle them,” vocalized Detective Kelly.

“Yes, yes, we are all aware of that possibility, Detective Kelly. For now, though, just solve this one and if it comes to it, we will see what we can do later,” suggested the sergeant.

Detective Kelly thought their conversation was over and almost began to get up. However, the sergeant continued, "But we will need regular progress reports with a suspect, descriptions, markings, and identifiable stuff. Between you and me, if we do not send out an APB out soon, the Police Chief might need someone to take the blame if this case is not solved quickly," informed the sergeant.

Detective Kelly paused, then looked at him with understanding, nodding as he thought about what exactly to omit from his notes of the briefing. "This war is in our neighborhood, Detective Kelly. End it fast. Dismissed," said the sergeant.

Detective Kelly got up and closed his notepad, then went to his desk. The day was far from over and he already had to begin working on this high-profile case. He had a feeling this was not going to be just another drug overdose case. These drug overdose cases were too sudden, and he felt the urgency from his superiors to solve it soon.

There must be more than one new drug organization in the city, surely. Detective Kelly began to wonder. How the fuck did this happen on my watch?

It was true. Crime like this in his city went through Detective Kelly first. Even small-time drug dealers on the block would have to make some contacts to start selling in that neighborhood;' just to avoid the detective's harsh justice. First, that fucking red stamp on the kilo of cocaine at the park and now these fucking addiction-pills!

Despite his profession preferred qualities, Detective Kelly was not a particularly patient man, though it sometimes did serve him well. His desire to get things done often found him on the side of action rather than reaction. Nothing illegal moves in this city without my cut!" thought Detective Kelly.

The detective took a long, hard look at his options. "Damn it! I got to get back to my street informants; or at least find me a hungry up and coming police officer. I will need some goddamn extortion money, too Fuck!" explained Detective Kelly.

Between finding the owners of the red chili pepper stamp and now this opioid threat, it felt like the detective was losing control of his city and extra income. He would need to change his strategy. The detective was thinking that it was some new drug organization that was responsible for the overdoses in the city, it was obvious. He assumed that it was some crime family, or even nothing but gangbangers that was behind this. Of course, they would have to be able to secure these very legal drugs without prescriptions. It was not as if they could simply steal their shipments or have an illegal trade. Messing with Big Pharm would be a no-no, so he hoped it would not extend that far up.

These new drug organizations will either pay me, die, or go to prison for a long time. Fuck it, I will do what I want even if they cooperate! It is too much money being made illegally in this city and I am not getting my fucking share, the detective thought in a rage.

*****

At St. Marks's Baptist Hospital, near the Hampton Heights neighborhood, a young Black woman entered an office. The name plate on the door read Angelita Dallas, Pharmacy. Director.

Angelita's office was decorated quite well, her accomplishments visible and on display. A Doctor of Pharmacy certificate was framed and on display behind the desk where Angelita would sit; clearly something about which she was proud. She had even finished her North American Pharmacist Licensure Examination (NAPLEX) along with her Delta XI PHI sisters with ease.

It was quite clear that Angelita was comfortable in her job. Always a leader, Angelita convinced seven of her sorority sisters to pilfer as many pills as possible of Oxycodone and Percocet for her on a weekly basis. Together the pills supply came up to a few hundred pills each week. Their amount, combined with her contribution of the same could easily give a few thousand per month for each prescription. This gave their group more than ten thousand pills monthly to sell at street value. Even with this amount, it was still hard for her drug organization to keep up with the city's demand for opioids. Especially in the Hampton Heights neighborhood.

Angelita's drug organization had perfect access to the prescription drugs being that they all had become directors at their respective hospitals. No one would suspect any of them of stealing pills. Each could simply explain the missing medication if necessary due to the large hospital pharmacy they supervised. The organization only supplied the pills being sold to one drug dealer. Therefore, there was limited access to them, which was why Angelita was so confident and so comfortable. To her, the operation was airtight.

Over the past two years this drug organization has profited over six million dollars and that sum was sure to increase in the future. All the drug organization's members have been employed at their respective hospitals for over ten years. Consequently, each had less than eight years for retirement. It was the perfect plan to sell drugs to add to their future retirement plans, at least to them. There was no overhead and an endless supply and clientele. No one would suspect them at all!

In the past, any missing medication was attributed to the pharmacy techs manually miscounting filled prescriptions for the inpatient units. There was theft by some of the young medication technicians that distributed medications overnight on the ICU and geriatric units. Mistakes were easy and excusable. However, it did make it into the medication log, something that they were accountable for; but they at least had solid stories to cover their tracks.

This morning Angelita felt extremely joyful. All her girls really came through for her. The pills were being delivered shortly from her sorority sisters. Should always depend on them to be on time, Angelita thought to herself. She will be meeting her street distributor later today. Angelita never really trusted men when it came to business. She felt that they were too ego-driven and lacked the emotional connection to genuinely care about others in an organization. "Most men only cared about themselves, and that behavior was not needed in her organization," thought Angelita.

Her distributor/drug dealer was a woman, too. Lisa Chin was her name. Angelita believed in one person distributing their pills and one person involved in supplying the product during handoffs. The fewer people involved besides her sisters, the better. This would lead to having less chance of her operation being discovered. She decided to call Lisa Chin to set up their rendezvous location.

"Lisa, how is your day? Are we still on for drinks after work honey," asked Angelita.

Lisa Chin listened to Angelita talk with a frown on her face. She hated that fake ass sunny disposition Angelita always displayed. She also knew that Angelita had street sense even though she came off as bougie.

To her, Angelita did not earn any respect from her. Lisa Chin felt Angelita did not have much experience in the real world, as she came from an upper middle-class family and always had a little more than the rest. She knew of Angelita from high school. She knew that the bitch was as fake as a wooden penny but made up for it with her wits and tenacity. Now, though, Angelita held all the cards, and all Lisa could do was play the game until she found a better supplier.

"Oh okay, so it is, honey. Yes, we will meet at the new restaurant located near the medical center. Be there at 7:00 pm."

Angelita was bewildered. Lisa was changing location. Not her character. "Okay sis, I will meet you there. Remember to bring your appetite." "Well honey, I am always hungry. Also, I got you that new tote bag you have been wanting for weeks now." "Great, I do love gifts! Especially if they come in huge boxes! See you soon!" Both ladies hung up their cellphones and resumed their daily activities.

Chapter 5
Suspicious Minds

The parking lot of Richard Kelly's car dealership was massive. He offered a wide selection of high quality new and used certified cars, trucks, and passenger vans. Customers could choose from such models as Mustangs, Expeditions, Pathfinders and Maximas, just to name a few, for their high-end needs. These vehicles were always the most coveted. There was something about American made muscle cars that just clicked with most of the people in the city.

Richard Kelly offered special financing or lease programs for both new and used vehicles at his dealership. True to his commercial promise; Richard Kelly accepted as little as $99.00 dollars down payment on any vehicle. Of course, the higher the price, the longer the payments lasted.

Today was an extremely busy Saturday morning for the car dealership. The new television advertising had really paid off for the Richard Kelly car dealership. Many people both in and out of the city came with no more than $100.00 dollars expecting to leave in a new Ford Expedition or a top-of-the-line Nissan.

Amongst the sea of customers was Little Ricky and one of his crew members. Little Ricky and his companion were just like the rest; looking to purchase a new vehicle with little down payment. They first walked directly to the Fords on display, both amazed by the luxury and all the optional amenities offered with the vehicle. There were car salespeople giving little 'tours' of each vehicle but Little Ricky and his friend opted to browse on their own.

Little Ricky sat inside one of the Fords. The young man turned on the stereo to examine the sound quality and marveled at the dark matte metallic exterior paint job. All the details that were especially important to any young man, and for Little Ricky, they were exactly how he wanted them.

However, the sound of the stereo was loud enough that even in the busy dealership lot, the sound system could clearly be heard by the customers, as well as the staff. The young man's actions caused unwanted attention and within moments two salespeople approached him in a professional manner.

"Good morning, gentlemen." One of them presented themselves to Little Ricky by the driver's seat window. "May I help you with your purchase of this fine new vehicle?" He put one of his hands on his hip and the other elbow on the roof of the car. "Do you want to buy this beautiful Ford? We only have five of these Expedition models left, and…as you can see…" He pointed towards the lot. "…you are not the only ones looking at this SUV."

Little Ricky was annoyed at the salesperson. It was his job, yes, but he just wanted to feel the steering wheel beneath his fingers. "No, no, we're just looking for now." Little Ricky told the salesperson, smiling with his teeth bared. "However," he began, "Do tell me about the down payment on this vehicle. I heard it was less than a hundred dollars. Is that true? I mean, what about the other shit? Credit checks and stuff? I heard on the TV you do not even need it," asked Little Ricky.

"Yes, that's right, sir. At Richard Kelly Ford and Nissan, your job is your credit." The salesperson said in a rehearsed speech. "Personally, I cannot speak on how it works or how it should work. It is just how it is done here. If you have the money and a pay stub, the vehicle is yours today to drive out of the lot."

Little Ricky laughed. "Damn, that's fucking great news, isn't it?" He turned his head towards his partner on the passenger seat. "Savion, call those two bitches you know with a job to come down here now! We are getting us a new car today my nigga!"

Both Little Ricky and Savion laughed. Savion got out of the vehicle and Little Ricky saw him walk to an isolated corner of the lot. Little Ricky got busy checking out the rest of the car while his friend pulled out his phone and made a call.

"So, do I start the paperwork for this Ford Expedition now?" the salesperson asked. He was getting anxious and wanted to get the deal completed. Richard Kelly would give him a piece of his mind if he spent too long not getting a sale.

"Hold up, nigga." Little Ricky took a while to answer, his face contorted in thought, as if he did not really want to follow through. "I changed my mind about the Expedition. Do you have any new minivans? I need something that is, how you would say, blacked out," asked Little Ricky.

The salesperson was surprised at the sudden and radical shift of vehicle selection but kept his cool. He surveyed the lot for minivans and looked back at Little Ricky, who continued. "You know, all black. Both the interior and exterior. The minivan also needs a dark tint and black rims. Do you have something like that in this big ass car dealership," asked Little Ricky as he looked around the lot, noticing a distinct lack of any such vehicle, but he was not worried.

"Of course, we do." The salesperson smiled. "Please follow me. We need to get to the back where we keep our special-order vehicles."

Little Ricky got out of the Ford, looked towards it with longing for a while before he took off after the salesperson. The walk was short, but as Little Ricky went to the back parking lot, he saw exactly what he wanted. Just then, Savion joined them as he saw them walking towards the back parking lot, running after them.

"Yo, the bitches will be here in 30 minutes. What cars are we going to buy today," asked his partner.

"Yo, I changed my mind about the Ford Expedition. It is too flashy and will cause unwanted attention. We are going to get two minivans instead. Both are better for what we need anyway." Savion's face showed a bit of confusion, but he often relied on Little Ricky to be the smarter one of the two. At least for now, therefore, Savion agreed. Both young men inspected the new presented vehicles. They played with the vehicles' interior gadgets as they waited for their lady friends to arrive with their pay stubs and to get the deal underway.

Due to the large turnout of potential customers, today was a more active Saturday morning. Even this early, it was busy, with in the commotion. Any other person would be hard pressed to be able to pay attention to any one person, let alone the tens or hundreds coming and going through the dealership. The new cars that had arrived, the ad, the down payment, and the extra sales put on by Richard Kelly had people coming in droves and taking cars away in massive quantities.

If everything went well, Alcia Adams would be able to edit the account books to avoid another audit from the IRS. There were two things in life about which Alcia was always considered, death, and taxes. Since death had not come, she would sure wish it had before the tax authorities did.

Before this big turn-out, Alcia had no idea how to prove that all the dealership's large profits were coming from vehicle sales, scheduled services, and repairs. Dealerships were a profitable business although the profit margins being high at the dealership even an amateur tax auditor could spot some clear errors in their account books. The receipts for these from past vehicle related charges did not add up at all. For now, Alcia planned to be very observant until she had a better understanding of the financial situation.

*****

The deaths of the two Mexican men at Robin Antonio Park were fresh in the mind on the Sandy Lopez. He was the leader of the Mexican drug organization that rivaled Richard Kelly. Sandy operated out of a large trailer park located on the outskirts of the city. He chose that location because of its isolation and rural environment. By the day, he owned a small landscaping company, though the cocaine drug sells were his main source of income. His low prices and high-quality drugs made him a formidable adversary to Richard Kelly, particularly because he did not like to be flashy about it.

Both drug organizations had moved to the area years ago after noticing the city was a prime location for drug distribution. However, unlike Richard Kelly, Sandy had little overhead. He had a small army of undocumented immigrant workers to move his drugs and enforce his rule. Sandy also had a nephew named AJ Black to launder his profits from his drug sales. It was never a perfect situation for Sandy Lopez, at least from his perspective, so he always assumed something would go wrong. That thought kept him grounded.

Today Sandy had enough intel to know that Little Ricky and his crew had killed his men during a drug deal gone wrong. He had ordered two of his men to follow the gang banger's every move for now. Sandy wanted to know their every breath, every bitch, and every single speck of cocaine they took from him was returned.

His real goal was to find out where Little Ricky hid the drugs and money. His men were already on the boy's trail and were waiting for the two people of interest to show up.

"Amigo (friend), where are those little cucarachas now?" Sandy spoke on his phone.

"Jefe (boss), they are at a car dealership." A voice answered from the other end, clearly Mexican. "You know, the one on TV, Richard Kelly Ford, and Nissan, to be exact. Can we get a new truck while we are here too?"

"Hell no! You must stay focused, amigo," ordered Sandy Lopez. His men liked to be a bit too efficient sometimes, and it was more work than Sandy had realized to keep them focused. "Those fuckers killed our campaneros and now they flaunt it in our faces by buying new vehicles with my fucking money!" Sandy shouted, but quickly composed himself. "Just continue to follow them for now. I need to know where they are keeping their stash and our property."

"You got it Jefe." The other man answered. "I just wanted a new truck, too. The one we drive is in bad need of repairs."

Damn it. Sandy thought. These men need a lesson on how to follow my fuckin' instructions. "Are you slow? Escucha (Listen to) me! We are not here for luxuries. Our job is to sell cocaine; not to show off. Now report back to me in four hours," yelled Sandy Lopez.

"Si Jefe, we will follow your directions. Da le (later)," the other man quickly answered. Sandy hung up the phone. "That little boy was going to get it, but for now, the only thing keeping him alive was his distance from the stash," thought Sandy.

Chapter 6
Never Too Much Surveillance

A semi-truck drove into a nearly abandoned industrial park just outside the city limits. It was raining that night, the water drops pouring onto the rusted iron and corroding concrete. The doors of the buildings had been closed shut with plywood. Corrugated **metal** and **sheets** of plastic covered what could be covered. Silence could be felt everywhere except for the occasional beat of thunder disturbing the peace.

The semi-truck was driven by a Black man named Bootsy. As the owner of a small independent trucking company, Bootsy had never been one to let others oversee what belonged to him. He did not like delegating to anyone high in the chain of command and he preferred being his own boss, too. That is why he never hired more than two drivers at a time to transport the long-distance cargo. His patience was too short for inexperienced drivers and untrustworthy individuals to work for him. There were a few occasions when Bootsy would take matters into his own hands, making deliveries himself; especially if it was some special cargo. Today was one of those special occurrences, with an equally special delivery. He was there to meet Sandy Lopez and deliver a large supply of cocaine.

Always cautious, Bootsy selected the drop-off locations for drug deliveries himself. He knew the ins and outs of the local terrain. Since it was such a sensitive fragile freight to transport. He preferred to be in familiar territory. Also, in his line of work Bootsy always had the odds in his favor because he never really had to show loyalty to any drug organizations. Whoever paid the best and agreed to his fair terms was able to get his transportation services. It was an arrangement that worked for him and his associates.

Bootsy's semi-truck came to a stop near a few men clearly waiting on his arrival to start the drug transaction. The engine of the truck shut off as it started to rain harder. Bootsy took a quick glance at the men and saw a face he had seen many times before, Sandy Lopez. He had met Sandy many times in the past and seeing him at a routine drug drop off was unusual. Most of the time it was Sandy's crew that did the drug handovers.

Bootsy exited his truck wearing his usual big smile on his face. He had a personality that everyone found to be warm and inviting. However, he could turn cold and dangerous at a moment's notice. If you remained in his good graces, you would be fine. Bootsy was also known for cracking jokes and not necessarily at anyone's expense either. He preferred to tell jokes that everyone would find funny. It was not unusual for Bootsy to have everyone around him laughing uncontrollably by the end of their conversation. Not to be mistaken Bootsy was all about having an enjoyable time, but he was also smart about his business. If you wanted to party Bootsy was your man. However, if you wanted to do business with him you would not find anyone more serious.

Bootsy walked up to Sandy Lopez and gave him a big manly hug. On any other occasion, Sandy would not allow this behavior, especially not during a drug deal. However, the two had conducted several transactions over the years and they grew fond of each other. Sandy had even invited Bootsy to

Mexico for a family trip. It was safe to say they were good acquaintances, if not friends, considering their business.

Seeing his acquaintance unfazed by the familiarity, Bootsy continued the good mood by cracking one of his jokes. As his humor was usually off the cuff and odd to most drug dealers he encountered, found the jokes funny.

"Jefe (boss), what is going on baby?" a smiling Bootsy asked Sandy. "I see the whole crew is here." Bootsy looked behind Sandy to scan his men. He noticed the men were calm, but still had rifles in hand ready to defend Sandy. "It is raining hard as hell out here! Bootsy continued; are you too cool for an umbrella loco? Where in the hell is your umbrella? Not even a hoodie man? With all this rain one of your boys might be made of sugar and melt!" Bootsy laughed and he saw that Sandy Lopez did too, with the grin he always had when talking to Bootsy.

"So, what are you saying my friend? One of my men is sweet like sugar. Cause only sugar melts in water." Sandy said teeth bared.

Despite the boss being on good terms, one of Sandy's men looked upset over Bootsy's joke. The man uttered something under his breath, trying to hide his expression as he did. But it was heard, even in the rain.

"Hold up now! Did one of your men say something to me?" Bootsy asked looking at the men standing behind Sandy Lopez. Bootsy asked again, "Do any of your men have something to say to me?" One of the Mexican men answered. "I was just talking to myself. I meant no disrespect." "Next time you start talking to yourself just tell yourself to shut the fuck up! You will live a lot longer if you do amigo," said Bootsy. Sandy's men knew that Bootsy could be an extremely dangerous man, if provoked. He had a reputation for being strict about his business when it came to making money and anyone who dared to try and rob him had just committed suicide. Bootsy's only weakness was young women and partying, which he enjoyed doing often. If anyone was willing to gamble messing with Bootsy, they had better know they were gambling with their lives.

Sandy and Bootsy suddenly laughed uncontrollably. They laughed for a good while before Sandy's men started joining in the laughter. As everyone continued to laugh, Bootsy's smile quickly faded as his face turned stoic and stoned. Whether it was a façade or real, Bootsy now had control of this situation and was now the most dangerous man in that abandoned industrial park.

Bootsy glanced up towards the roof of the warehouse before he continued with the drug transaction and Sandy's men eased up as well. "All bullshit aside, let us unload the product," said Bootsy as he pointed towards his truck. "I must get home before the local news comes on at 11 pm." Sandy Lopez turned towards his men and gestured them to continued. "You folks heard the man. Let us move the product out the trailer in record time today."

Both men walked away from the trailer while Sandy's men unloaded the product. They walked towards an awning covered with some metal sheets that gave them a dry location for the time being. It was perfect to talk without others hearing their conversation. While they waited for the job to be completed, a conversation started between them.

"Bootsy, I did not think you were the news watching kind of guy." Sandy began, looking at his friend. "How else would I know where to avoid these young thugs looking to rob me? I heard what happened to your men on the news. I cannot let the shit happen to me. That is why I am always moving locations." Bootsy said. "That is what I love about you, my friend. You are never predictable. If only you would just work for me exclusively. You could own one hundred new semi-trucks," Sandy replied.

Bootsy answered quickly, "No thank you my friend. I do not want the spotlight. Leave that shit to the young boys like your nephew."

"Do you mean AJ?" Sandy asked, rhetorically. Sandy started thinking about his nephew. AJ was a good kid he thought and smart. In Sandy's opinion his nephew was the kind of person that could be useful to his drug organization. Sandy was always looking to launder his drug profits.

Sandy finally responded to Bootsy mentioning his nephew. "Bootsy, I know what you are about to say but AJ and I have already had that talk and he promised to scale back on the flashing of money."

"Well, from what I saw at the gentlemen's club last night; you folks need to have another talk," Bootsy replied. "That motherfucker paid for everyone's bottles of champagne in the VIP section. It was like a damn Al Pacino movie in there last night. Big Boss style" Bootsy said.

Sandy Lopez looked at Bootsy with his face contorted. "That fucker did what? Tough love must be used on my sobrino (nephew). He does not listen worth a shit!" "These young boys are hardheaded," Sandy said.

"Yes, amigo. Now, tell me, whatever the hell that word means. Sobrino? That is an unfamiliar word to add to my Spanish list! Does that mean mother fucker in Spanish or something like that," Bootsy said while laughing. "I was in the club last night translating pimping on my phone with these two young Dominican whores that work there. We could hear AJ bragging about his money at the bar from the VIP section. He got to be more careful," Bootsy advised.

"That sounds like him." Sandy said, ignoring the first part of his question about Spanish words. Sandy had more important matters to investigate and his mind was already in a different place. "But what do you mean by translating pimping? Is that something new," Sandy asked Bootsy.

"It was new to me too, but the game has changed! Now it is my go-to for bilingual pimping!" Bootsy said. "See, I do not speak Spanish very well and they speak little to no English. So, I use the translate app on my phone to pick up women, you see. I say something to my phone, pass it to the bitches to read and they do the same in reverse. Bam!" Bootsy exclaimed, clapping his hands together as he said the last part.

Sandy Lopez could not help but laugh. It was just like Bootsy to go after pussy like this. "That is fucking genius. Where was that thing when I first arrived in the country? I could have truly used it. I would not have all these damn ass baby mamas looking to get some of what I got," Sandy said while laughing.

Both men laughed as they walked back to the semi-truck trailer. Sandy's men were just finishing unloading the drugs and taking inventory of what had been delivered. Bootsy once again looked up towards the roof of the warehouse. Just a glance, long enough to see what he needed to see, but short enough length that even if someone were watching him, his glance would go unnoticed.

Bootsy made a few more jokes as he said his goodbyes to Sandy and the rest of the men. Bootsy soon stepped back in his semi-truck and drove off in the misty rain. Once he was safely away from the industrial park, Bootsy made a phone call to his clandestine partner positioned on the roof of a warehouse back there. It would have been obvious to anyone that Bootsy did not get his reputation by accident. However, Sandy and his crew were unaware that Bootsy was not alone. He had someone watching the entire deal transaction from the roof of one of the buildings in the industrial park.

Bootsy's watchful eye on the proverbial roof, as it were, was in constant communication with him through an earpiece. It was raining and Bootsy being him, had concealed the equipment by wearing his hoodie over his head. No need to excuse himself for wearing his hoodie up in the rain.

Bootsy's partner used the scope of their rifle to get a bird's eye view of the drug transaction. The person informs him of everyone's movements and if necessary, eliminate anyone if needed. Being prepared in their line of work was not just a good thing but necessary. Therefore, Bootsy making it out of today's drug transaction safely was not by accident.

"Is everything cool Sophia? I do not have anything to worry about, do I? Bootsy asked on the phone. Sophia answered, the sound of rain unmistakable from her end of the line. "No cousin, everything is cool. Sandy and his men just left and seem incredibly pleased with themselves. That is another easy payday for us, for sure. I will meet you at the spot later tonight." "Bet." Bootsy replied. Wait Sophia; I need to make a stop at Walmart and buy another prepaid cellphone. Remember to replace your cellphone every month. Hell, even my own big brother does not have my cell phone number. I got to call his ass on the regular to stay connected, you know." "Shit, I know!" Sophia said laughing. "You need to call him soon after replacing your cell. We are due for a vacation in Miami. It always feels like summer there. I am so ready to get out of here to relax and chill." "You're right, Sophia." Bootsy said as he drove. "Can you believe he gave all this money up just to get married? Not us, we will always stay single Sophia. Being single is the shit my girl!" Bootsy laughed. Sophia did too, but she had to stay focused on her job for just a little longer. She remained on site until Sandy and his crew left the industrial park.

Sophia Fire was Bootsy's closest friend, roommate, and enforcer. She used her beauty and knowledge of the drug game to help Bootsy accumulate his wealth. She was slightly older than Bootsy and had no family nearby. She was the kind of friend who was very protective of Bootsy and tolerated no disrespect from anyone. She enjoyed his humor but appreciated his work ethic even more. They both lived in a rural area outside of the city by choice. Bootsy reason was 'the ability to see your enemies coming from afar.' His location was strategically chosen to eliminate any threats. Their property had two houses, its own water source, and live animals. To the average eye they were simple country folks and that was exactly what they wanted. To Bootsy and Sophia, it was a defendable location if push ever came to a shove, or worse.

Chapter 7
Money Thicker Than Blood

The morning was cloudless, with blue skies and a pleasant sun. It looked like the town had been freshly washed, like it had gotten a chance for a new life. However, the tranquil scenery was not on Sandy Lopez's mind as his car stopped in Soapy Wash laundromat's parking lot. The laundromat was a clandestine place of business for Sandy that did not need to be documented.

Sandy arrived early that morning for a meeting with his nephew, AJ Black. Sandy had set up this meeting to discuss AJ's excessive spending of their organization's drug profits in public places. Sandy's earlier conversation with Bootsy had revealed that AJ had not listened to his earlier warning and consequences of spending large sums of money at local venues. Sandy watched as AJ scanned the laundromat parking lot. AJ did a quick once over of the entire parking lot before he slowly walked towards Sandy's car.

AJ Black entered his uncle's car a little confused about this unplanned meeting. AJ operated as Sandy's money launderer for his drug operations. He was also Sandy's nephew, his youngest sister's son. AJ's father was a Black man. AJ carried his father's last name. Sandy used his nephew's American last name to assist him in acquiring businesses and property without causing suspicion from the authorities. However, Sandy never let his nephew's mixed heritage alter his love for him. Sandy treated AJ as his own son.

AJ had obtained his master's degree in accounting from Hampton University and was at the top of his graduating class. His bi-racial makeup made him known to many as a pretty boy with his copper tone skin complexion and curly black hair. He owned several laundromats, beauty salons, and barber shops in the area. All were used successfully to launder money for Sandy Lopez's drug organization; all of AJ's businesses were cash only. All the business was lucrative. So, Sandy tolerated some of AJ's spending excessive habits and unwanted attention.

Despite his being told in the past to stop his erratic behavior, AJ Black continued. Sandy grows weary of continuously reminding AJ that his actions were not conducive to their drug organization. "In fact," Sandy told his nephew. "They are detrimental. Do you know what that means, boy?

Det-ri-mental! Put that education to work and get smart about it!" AJ Black was smart and liked to show it off too. However, bashful young men like AJ always showed off too much around the wrong people. The places AJ frequently visited did not invite the most upstanding of men or women.

Today Sandy was in no mood for AJ's usual mental games. He wanted some answers from AJ, and they had better be good. "Good morning Unc!" AJ said, as he entered the car. "Why are we meeting so damn early in the morning; there's still frost on the car windows."

Sandy Lopez waited before answering. He usually waited to see if his nephew would think before he spoke. However, AJ clearly had not learned any lesson. "Your black side of you is starting to show. We Mexicans get up at dawn." "We try to get our work done before it gets too hot as the day progresses," said Sandy.

"Wow Unc!" AJ got defensive. Sandy did not like it when AJ did not listen. "You are starting to sound a little racist to me! AJ continued, Anyway, what is up? We both know everything is going as planned with the businesses. I will have the $400,000.00 you gave me yesterday cleaned up by this Friday. All the funds will be deposited next week during our usual monthly bank runs," explained AJ.

Sandy Lopez sighed. "Damn, you cannot take a joke, nephew. No, I am not racist. Hell, I am looking for a Black woman now to have a baby." Sandy said, trying to ease the tension. "You know, I think black mixed with another race always makes beautiful kids." He said, giving his nephew a pat on his shoulder.

"Now, let us talk about you making it rain again at the gentlemen's club." AJ facial express became serious he prepared for what was coming. "I told you before that you cannot flash your wealth around in a small city like this one. It will cause too much attention from the police officers or even the federal government. Hungry niggas will target you to rob. Consider this my last warning!" Sandy barked.

"Uncle, I just needed to blow off some steam." AJ spoke like a child justifying themselves to their parents. "I mean, you had me move to this country ass city where everybody knows each other and there are only three clubs within fifty miles radius. Also, with the rate we are moving money from the drugs, I can never take a vacation. I mean really, what is the use in having money if you cannot spend it on shit," AJ asked?

"AJ, the people we work for do not tolerate mistakes." Sandy Lopez informed. "You are putting all our lives at risk with your dumbass behavior. Our bosses will kill us, your mother, and anyone else you love just to prove a point!" Sandy raised his voice, just enough to let his nephew know he was concerned but not enough to convey anger. "Now, you accepted this role to launder our money so do your damn job."

"Uncle, it is hard to explain to the banks how our businesses can generate over $800,000 per month in profits without causing suspicion. That is profits uncle, not the total! Even some successful businesses do not do that! Especially in this small city! So, sometimes I spend a little money just to keep our deposit amounts consistent, Unc," AJ explained.

Sandy Lopez sighed. AJ was too smart for his own good. AJ had this ego and part of it was deserved. However, it was so obvious that he did not comprehend his uncle's warning.

"That is understandable, AJ. Your job as our money launderer is to do three things. You need to keep account of the money we dropped off to you, clean the money and deposit it into the bank accounts as if the funds were profits from our businesses; that is, it. You must convert our profits into assets. Make the deposits into the business bank accounts regularly to not cause suspicion. So, get your shit together. It is not your money you are spending," yelled Sandy.

AJ Black started looking nervous, speaking quickly. "I do that, uncle. I never miss a deposit. You know that."

"Let me fucking finish, Mr. Master's degree!! Sandy exclaimed, loudly and angrily. AJ was silent in the car. "Let me reiterate again you are here for three things. That is money placement, layering, and integration. You must layer the money into multiple transactions. So let me explain this to you for the last time. Now listen. You transfer funds over multiple bank accounts and purchase expandable items like artwork, real estate, and vehicles for the landscaping company. These funds are not for you to be spending on damn expensive cars, jewelry, and strippers!" Sandy spoke loudly.

"I only do that rarely. That should not cause suspicion. Everybody flexes on hoes, Unk," AJ said proudly.

Sandy Lopez slapped AJ hard across his face because he had enough of AJ trying to justify his excessive spending rather than apologizing for his actions. "I warned you not to interrupt me. The next time you do that I will not stop hitting you," clarified.

"Now, the last part is the integration of the money. This is the part I am not seeing you do. You must reenter the profits back into the local economy. Invest in local companies or start a bogus charity. In fact, start a charitable organization immediately and place us on the Board of Directors. By doing this you can legitimately spend copious amounts of money because we can give ourselves large salaries as board members. Dividends, AJ! Dividends! This will justify our wealth to the authorities, understand?" asked Sandy.

AJ Black waited before answering, his face showing a clear smugness and anger. However, he was trying to hide it. "May I talk now, uncle?" AJ asked and Sandy nodded his approval. "I understand completely now, and I will start the paperwork for a non-profit charity today. I will not let you down," said AJ Black.

"You better not fuck this situation up nephew." Sandy Lopez said to him; "for all our sakes." Sandy sighed, looking out towards the road, seeing all the cars coming and going. A few cars have now started to park in the laundromat parking lot. Both knew it was time to end their meeting. "Now, get out of my car. Ponte las Pilas! (Get your act together!) I have a landscaping job to do," said Sandy.

AJ Black left his uncle's car and walked towards his office located at the rear of the laundromat. He went in and watched his uncle leaving the parking lot through his office window. Once AJ was sure that his uncle was far enough away from the parking lot, he immediately made a phone call.

"Did you folks hear all that?" AJ asked on the phone. He did not wait for a response. "I hope that is enough evidence for you. Now, you people promised that my mother and I will not be charged with any crimes, right?" Someone spoke on the other end and AJ nodded to himself in agreement. "Okay, I will see you later tonight. Bye," AJ said as he hung up the phone.

AJ could not help but wonder how he got himself into this terrible situation. However, it was too late to return to a life of normalcy that he once had. All he had to do now, was continue being AJ Black, the man who cleans dirty money for his uncle's drug organization.

Chapter 8
A Boastful Night

11 Months Earlier

*****

AJ Black continued spending large sums of money in the VIP section of Daddy's Playhouse. The gentlemen's club was one of the largest and most famous (or infamous) ones in the city. The club catered to anyone that wanted to mingle with the underbelly of the city. Daddy's Playhouse was a good place to start. It is where the people that got taken advantage of were found and the people taking advantage over them as well. Of course, as it was always the place to be seen if you want attention.

Tonight, AJ was extra raucous. He bragged to the dancers and to others in the VIP section about his status in Sandy's drug organization. It seemed the more alcohol he consumed the more details of the drug organization AJ provided to anyone that would listen.

He was talking to the server, loudly; enough that it was no longer a private conversation between just AJ and the server. "Hi beautiful!" AJ exclaimed. It was already necessary to speak loudly because of all the music blaring in the club. However,

AJ was recklessly loud. "Close off the VIP section for the next hour, baby," AJ ordered.

"Now, why would I do that?" the server asked, putting her hands on her hips. "This club is packed, and everybody is spending money!" She pointed to several guests enjoying themselves, talking to the dancers and their friends.

"You must be new here." AJ replied, his voice clearly hoarse; his breath smelling of alcohol. "Just in case you do not know, I am the richest motherfucker in here!" AJ raised the bottle he held it to the crowd. "I am paying for all the drinks in this section for the next hour, baby!" The crowd cheered, and some banged on the tables to show their appreciation. AJ waited for the fanfare to die down a bit. "Now, bring everybody bottles of champagne and not the cheap shit either. Bring us the Jontue' Marci champagne!! We are only drinking the best tonight!!"

"My bad daddy!" The server replied, her voice more playful now. "I will get some help to bring out the Jontue' Marci bottles. Now, do not forget about your servers when it is time to pay the bill."

AJ laughed. "Baby, you can write down your tip. Believe me, you cannot hurt my bank account." AJ had to stammer through his words. "Also, bring me and those gentlemen sitting at the table next to me your most expensive cigars! You can also tell the first-string dancers that the big ballers have arrived. Tell them I am looking for them to do something strange for a little piece of change."

"I think everybody back in the VIP section heard you, sugar!" responded the server, "Word to the wise. Please be careful spending all this money. You know there are plenty of wolves in here tonight and you are looking like something to eat." The server eyed AJ up and down, deliberate in her lack of subtlety.

"Shit…" AJ looked at the people in the VIP section. "These motherfuckers know not to fuck with me. My family runs all the dope in this city. If they rob me tonight, they will die before morning and that you can believe, baby," said AJ.

"Okay big spender, your orders of Jontue' Marci and the dancers are on the way to the VIP section. Please be safe and enjoy yourself," said the server. Her playful demeanor died down a bit, being more straight forward now.

"Thank you, sexy." AJ said, bringing himself closer to the server. "Now let me ask you a question. Do you have any condoms for sale? I need the largest you got. I can tell it is going to be one of those nights," whispered AJ.

The server got into her playful manner, and giggled. "Okay it's like that daddy." She reached behind the counter but did not pull anything out just yet. She waited, seeing AJ's reaction and pulled out a large black packet, with a round shape bulging outward. "The condoms that you need will be Magnum-sized. How many do you want," asked the server.

"You better give me five for tonight and please be quick about it. Those pills I took an hour ago are starting to kick in. I feel X-rated. Hell no, triple X rated baby!" AJ voice was getting back to being a bit too loud for the subject of the conversation.

The server handed AJ five condoms and proceeded to get the rest of his order. Meanwhile, AJ's brash and less-than-subtle talking got the attention of the two larger gentlemen sitting at the table next to him. The men were eager to talk to AJ Black and they thanked him for ordering the champagne for everybody.

"Thank you for getting everybody the best shit at the bar. Good of you to do. Jontue Marci is the best shit champagne there is." One of the large men said. "Honestly, I have seen people close off the VIP section before they usually order a few Hennessey bottles and nudge everyone else to fuck off. You, my guy, just spent over $10,000.00 on bottles. Now, that is balling out of control."

"That is showing real love my guy. Real love." The second man added. "My name is Synell, my friend's name is Julian. We are just here visiting from Miami, and we did not expect any ballers in this small ass city." The second man switched between looking at his friend and AJ. "Say, this shows that there is money being made in a major way here. Do you mind if we join you at your table in the VIP section?"

AJ stood up from his table and shook hands with the men as they sat down together.

Julian, the man who had approached AJ Black first, started talking. "Now, the least I can do is buy food for the rest of these people too. What would you like us to order? This is our first time visiting this club. What tastes good?"

"Hah!" AJ laughed while a spoke. "Nice to meet you and yes, the food here slaps and I am hungrier than a motherfucker too. I normally order some grilled chicken wings, lamb chops, and sampler platters. Just order that for each table. That will take care of the food for the VIP section for sure.

"I'm on it!" Synell added as he called one of the servers and made the order. Julian leaned closer to AJ, toning his voice down. "Yo, while my man is ordering the food let us chop it up about what you do around here. We could not help but hear you telling the server that your family is running the drug business around here and I think we can help each other."

AJ Black paused. He thought for a moment. He decided it was best to simply play dumb. "Nah, my brother. You heard that all wrong. We run a landscaping business in this city. That is what I said to her." AJ's voice had gotten much more balanced and regular, no longer stammering through his words."

"Well, that is a shame." Julian replied, looking down a bit, before adding. "Because we need a new drug source. I was hoping that you were the answer to our dilemma."

"Sorry, my man." AJ answered. "But no need to be down, brother! We can still pop these bottles of Jontue Marci champagne, get our grub on, and touch these bitches!" As AJ said that a few strippers entered the VIP section. "Here come the first stringers now. Hi Sexy Red! I have been waiting for you all night," said AJ as he smiled.

"Well, the wait is over daddy." Sexy Red replied. She was one of AJ's favorites. "Do you have condoms this time? You know it is best to be safe, boo! I am not trying to get pregnant, baby." She moved her hips and added a bit of sultriness to her voice.

AJ pulled the condoms out his pocket, showing them to Sexy Red. "Look baby, I am so ready!"

"I see that." Sexy Red replied, pushing herself closer to AJ to show her assets a bit more. "You plan on being here all night with that many condoms?"

"Oh, the condoms are for you and two more of the finest bitches in here that you want to fuck with me." AJ replied, smirking and smiling. "You go pick the two girls while I drink this bottle of champagne and eat some chicken wings. I need something in my stomach after I take my pills."

"You got it daddy." Sexy Red answered. "I know of two girls in here I have been waiting to fuck anyway. Are we going with you for the rest of the night," she asked.

"Yeah! I got a condominium downtown. I need all three of you girls for the rest of the night. We are about to do some wild shit! Are you ready," asked AJ.

Two more strippers entered the VIP section per Sexy Red's request. Both walked up next to her and kissed her in full view of everyone. "Okay, that will be $4,500.00 for all of us. Give us 30 minutes to get our belongings. I will signal you when we are ready to leave the club," said Sexy Red.

AJ Black was feeling particularly happy by this news. "Sexy Red, make it an even $5,000.00. You can keep the extra $500.00 for yourself. Just make sure the girls are into some freaky shit.

"Absolutely, let me set everything up for you now. "Eat up! You are going to need your energy boo!" Sexy Red said as she smacked each of the girls on the backside, who giggled with her. See you in about 30 minutes baby." Sexy Red sauntered off with the two strippers.

AJ Black admired Sexy Red walking away. Although the two large gentlemen wanted to continue their previous conversation, AJ was no longer in the mood to talk to them. He had love on his mind and did not want to be around people when he was like that.

"Like my friend was saying before Sexy Red brought her fine ass out here." Synell began. "We can always use a new plug. I hope you can be that for us?"

AJ Black having his mind elsewhere was munching down on some food instead of answering the man. It was convenient for AJ that Sexy Red showed up when she did. "If you need a hookup on getting your grass cut in Miami, then I am your man. Other than that, let me enjoy this champagne and get a lap dance before I leave here. Shit, I already paid for the champagne and cigars," said AJ. He was the only one that knew Sexy Red had told him to wait thirty minutes until she returned with the other strippers. He was using her as an excuse to leave the VIP section and not converse with the men any further. AJ informed the men that he had to use the restroom to make a quick exit.

AJ waited a while in the restrooms, washing his hands and face before he walked towards the women now waiting for him by the bar with a devilish smile. AJ grabbed one of them by their ass and started walking towards the exit. As the group began walking out the exit door, AJ's arm was grabbed by one of the large men he had been talking to in the VIP section earlier.

AJ turned towards the man. It was Synell who had grabbed his arm. "We have not finished talking to you. Step back into the men's restroom for a minute. Let me holla at you quick. You are not going anywhere until we are finished talking. Ya heard," said Synell.

AJ Black immediately tried to maneuver himself from the man's tight hold. "Hold on brother. Do not fucking grab me like that in front of my bitches, all rough and shit! Now get your big ass hands off me, back up a little and then we can talk inside the restroom," AJ said angrily at the man. However, he had sobered up enough after eating some food and realized these men were serious.

AJ walked towards his girls and addressed his prize girl. "Here Sexy Red," he handed her the keys. "You ladies get in my car and wait for me. This shit will not take too long. They got me fucked up! I will not be long baby girl," informed AJ.

"Okay daddy." Sexy Red replied as she took the keys off him and directed the other strippers towards AJ's car. "Stay focused while you are there. We had never seen those guys before in this club. Let me know if you need me to call security," said Sexy Red. She knew the men were trying to strongarm AJ and they were not messing around.

"No baby, I'm good!" AJ Black replied, looking over his shoulder. "You sexy ladies go ahead and wait for me. Start stretching like you are about to run a mother fucking marathon cause tonight we are about to do some Olympic style crazy shit!" AJ smacked her on the ass. "How you say it boo? Now on your mark…get set…and get your ass to the car!"

The ladies walked towards AJ's car laughing and he followed the two men as they entered the restroom.

"Now, what part of I DO NOT sell drugs do you guys do not understand?" AJ started off, not even looking around to see if anyone else was in there. "Are you motherfuckers slow or something? Do you have a learning disorder? Did not I…"

Julian almost immediately punched AJ in the stomach. "Shut the fuck up little man! Now like my friend told you earlier, our conversation was not over. Your name is AJ Black," said Julian.

AJ looked stunned. "I never told you, my name. What is this about? Who are you and what do you want with me?"

Synell grabbed AJ by his shirt. "It's about us having enough evidence to put your hoe ass away for a good 30-year in prison, AJ! We know all about your money laundering for your uncle's drug organization. We have been following you for months now. I am FBI agent Synell Black, and this is FBI agent Julian Brandon." They both took out their badge. It was standard procedure for them to show their badge. They made a habit of only showing their badges briefly, never letting the other person read any details. It was a common tactic both men used to gain some power over their conversation with criminals.

"You folks have the wrong fucking man," said AJ. He was defending himself, knowing he was caught, but also knowing he could not do anything about it. "All my businesses are 100% legal. I have done nothing wrong. Now, let me get the fuck out of this restroom. I have pussy waiting on me in the car, "explained AJ.

Julian was not buying AJ's story of earning money legitimately, not one bit. "You are going to play that 'I do not know shit' game with us? Well, let us see if your mother is going to play the same game when we arrest her ass tonight," told Julian.

AJ Black was shocked. "For what?" he asked, his eyes and face betraying the tough guy look he tried to present. "My mother did not do shit! You fucking Feds will do anything to get an arrest won't you? I have not done shit and neither has she. I do not know who you were watching and following, but it was not me or my mother!" yelled AJ.

Synell reached into his jacket and bought out some photos. AJ instantly recognized the woman in the pictures. "If she is so damn innocent, then why is she in this photo handing drugs to an undercover agent? Why are you in this other photo taking large sums of money from Sandy Lopez? A known drug cartel lieutenant from Mexico, isn't he? That is, you, isn't it?" Synell flipped through the photos, adding insult to injury as he spoke.

AJ Black laughed sarcastically. "Wow, so every Mexican small business owner is a drug cartel lieutenant now. I understood the assignment when I started working for my uncle. However, you folks are threatening me with arresting my mother. That is some low shit to do! We all know that she was not responsible for delivering any drugs. You folks photoshopped that damn photo to frame her just to arrest me?"

"Don't flatter yourself AJ." Synell replied. "We don't want you. We want your damn uncle. You are not worth shit, now either you will agree to help us and be able to go home with those young ladies or you can go to jail tonight. Then you must worry about some mass murdering men asking you if you do any freaky shit too in prison," said Synell.

AJ Black knew he was backed into a corner. He was not going to play the hero today and take all the criminal charges. AJ was not going to sacrifice his life for the sake of his uncle's drug organization. "Well, that choice is easy. When and where do we meet tomorrow to discuss our new business arrangement gentlemen? I am not about to be no man's bitch. I can get freaky but not with boy bussy."

Julian and Synell looked at each other, surprised. "Damn, this was easier than I thought. Hah! That is a record for agreeing to the deal! He is soft as shit. No hint of thug at all in his bones" Synell said while smiling. "They do not make thugs like they used to. AJ Black, just meet us at your office at 9am tomorrow morning," said Julian. AJ straightened his shirt as he exited the restroom. "That will give me enough time to clean up after fucking those whores," said AJ.

Julain spoke to AJ Black as he reached the restroom hallway. "And do not forget we are following your every move. Just assume that everything you say is recorded. Now, you can go to your bitches and tell them anything you like on how you controlled this conversation, and we will play along."

"Okay motherfuckers, like I said, talk to me tomorrow." AJ Black said to them as the men walked out behind him. "I have no time for business now. These are not my office hours. Meet me at my office. Right now, I got my mind on some pussy. See you motherfuckers in the morning or whenever I get there."

As AJ Black left the building looking puzzled, he wondered how he was going to get out of this situation. It was apparent that was not going to let his mother or himself go to prison. However, turning informant on his uncle was like committing suicide. AJ would have to think fast and smart to get out of this situation alive.

Chapter 9
No Escaping This

A red sports car sped off the I-85 freeway off ramp. The car quickly turned onto the less traveled Boyd highway and continued to pick up speed. In her haste, the driver did not notice a police cruiser making chase. However, it was not a highway patrol officer, but a regular metro police car pursuing the vehicle. Police officer Cynthia Brown was conducting a speed check on this remote section of Boyd highway. This section was located close to Robin Antonio Park where two dead Mexican men had been found murdered. Therefore, this area was a place of interest for the local police.

Always one to follow orders. Cynthia Brown monitored every vehicle's speed as she hid from the driver's view while looking for speed violators. She had recently transferred from her pervious police department to enhance her career. However, Cynthia's sudden transfer to the local police department had many of her fellow officers leery of her because of how quickly she was making arrests. Cynthia's arrest record was getting her noticed by her superiors and this rubbed some officers the wrong way. In her brief time at the police department, she had managed to recruit many informants to assist her in arresting criminals left and right. She was a petite woman with blonde hair and a muscular frame. Cythina was too much of a do-gooder to be taken seriously by most of her fellow officers. However, she could display a harsh attitude with skill when provoked. Still considered a newlywed by most, Cythina had been married for four years.

Cynthia's commitment to her job made her even deal with average car speedsters in a by the book manner; she was always a stickler for the rules. She was never going to let a speedster go with a warning just because of their wealth or status in the local community. Cynthia was now quickly picking up speed while pursuing the red sports car. She turned on her sirens and continued to chase.

In the driver's seat of the red speeding car sat Arrferria Carson, a pharmacy director at one of the local hospitals. The music in the sports car was blaring; the speakers would have shaken anyone inside if someone were accompanying her. Arrferria was texting someone on the phone while speeding. That was a double whammy for anyone driving recklessly. If she had not been texting, she would have noticed the police cruiser following her.

The flashing lights of the sirens were unmistakable and as they catch Arrferria's eyes she quickly panicked. She almost dropped the phone and losing control of the red sports car. Once she regained control of the car and her composure, she became nervous. Arrferria knows that this traffic stop will not go well for her since she is transporting eight hundred pills of Oxycodone and Percocet. They are not exactly well-hidden, either. Why would they? Arrferria is a pharmacy director carrying medicine. What would be suspicious about that, right, she thought.

However, Arrferria did not want to take any chances. She looked for a discreet location to dispose of the drugs before the police could notice. She slowed the car just enough preparing to throw the drugs out the window. Arrferria made a mental note of where she would throw the drugs so she could come back and get them later, or at least, that was the plan. Before Arrferria could make the throw another police car from the opposite direction stopped their car in front of Arrferria's sports car causing her to step on her brakes immediately.

Arrferria had a defeated look on her face as a police officer approached her car. She was too scared to even realize that the music was still playing loudly. Her car's window was rolled down as she watched police officer Cynthia Brown walked towards the driver's side of her car.

"Please turn off your music and provide me with your license, registration, and proof of insurance, ma'am. Why are you in such a hurry today, Miss," Cynthia Brown asked with one of her hands holding a notepad and her other on her hip, close to her holster.

Arrferria Carson took a deep breath and cleared her throat. "I did not realize that I was a speeding officer. Can I just get a warning this time? I am just getting off a long shift at work and I just want to go home. I do apologize, Sis," she said as the officer looked over her documents.

Cynthia was annoyed at that last remark. She braced for another classic speech of sisterhood and sisterly love that female speeders often try to use to get out of their speeding violations. Cynthia did not want to deal with the rabbling today. "Well, for one, I am not your Sis. Now since you were going fifty miles over the speed limit, I am going to have to arrest you for reckless driving. Now, please step out of your car slowly."

"Are you fucking serious? Arrest me!? Can I just get a speeding ticket? "Anferria exclaimed with a mixture of panic, shock, and anger in her voice. "I need to get home to my children. This is ridiculous!"

"Ms. Carson, you need to calm down and speak to me in a non-threatening way moving forward or I will be forced to use my stun gun. Do you understand," Cynthia asked loudly and clearly.

Arrferria took a few deep breaths to regain her composure. "There is no need to use excessive force, officer. I am complying with your orders! An arrest is overdoing it, don't you think? I was just driving a little over the speed limit. I am no criminal, no need to arrest me like one!" Arrferria got out of the car with her hands up. "I am in fear of my safety as a Black woman by your threats. Let me get my phone to record this. This is absurd," Arrferria said as she reached for her bag located inside her car.

"Your concerns are noted." Cynthia Brown replied, in a clear, dry voice. "Now place your hands behind your back and spread your legs. I am placing you under arrest for reckless and excessive driving as you were driving at a speed of 95 mph in a fifty-mph speed zone. You could have killed someone."

"Come on now. I was not going that damn fast." Arrferria said as the officer cuffed her. "Why did you put the handcuffs on me so damn tight? This is police brutality. Please stop pushing me so hard into the police car. I want to call my lawyer!" screamed Arrferria.

Cynthia Brown did not answer. She knew Arrferria would get her opportunity for a phone call to a lawyer once she was at the police station.

"I am going to leave you in the back seat while I check your vehicle. Now is there anything in the vehicle that I need to be aware of, like a gun, or anything of the sort? Drugs, maybe?"

Arrferria froze. "Wait- a- minute." Arrferria stammered. "Why do you need to check my car for anything? Why would you say I have drugs in my car? I am already in your custody and inside the police car! You do not have my permission!"

Arrferria shouted at Cynthia as she went towards her sports car.

"So, you are hiding something in there, are you? Why are you so nervous? I am going to call for more backup. Should I inform our narcotics officer to bring the department's canine to search your car now?" Cynthia waited midway between her police cruiser and Arrferria's own car.

"Narcotics? No, no, damn." Arrferria closed her eyes, thinking about what her next steps would be. "Just let me call my lawyer. I do not deserve to be treated in this manner. I am an educated woman, a homeowner who pays taxes that pays your salary." Cynthia grabbed a radio from her hip and spoke something that Arrferria could not really make out. All she could hear was a faint '10-4' by the end before Cynthia put her radio back and began checking the car's exterior.

The narcotics officer arrived at the traffic stop within 15 minutes, accompanied by a canine in a police vest. Arrferria rapidly knew what the officer would discover and the nervousness on her face was palpable. The canine instantly began barking and the officers knew that something was up. They found a large package of pills, unmarked and in a clear bag. However, it was not long before the narcotics officer recognized them as opioids.

Cynthia Brown called the senior detective that was on the opioids case, Detective Kelly, to inform him of this drug bust. Detective Kelly had asked all the police officers at the precinct to contact him if any illegal opioids were found, as he had an been leading the ongoing case of two teens dying of overdoses recently.

"Hello," a groggy detective's voice answered on the other end of the line.

"Detective Kelly" said Officer Brown just pulled over a lady speeding on Boyd highway and she had a sizable number of illegal opioids in her possession. I am going to turn them into the evidence department when I arrive at the station with the driver of the car. I just thought you should know."

"Excellent job, Officer Brown complimented Kelly. However, I am near your location. I can turn in the drugs. You just ensure the driver is booked and wait for me to interrogate her at the police station. You can stay around for the interrogation if you like."

Cynthia Brown was a bit confused. This was not standard protocol. "Are you sure that you do not want me to turn in the evidence and the driver? That is against protocol," asked Cynthia.

"Just do what I ask you to fucking do officer Brown, and that is an order!" shouted Detective Kelly as he approached the traffic stop location.

"Relax detective, I see you pulling up. The drugs are still in the driver's car. I am taking her down to the precinct for booking now. Also, I would love to be a part of this interrogation, you know, get to see the experts at work," requested Cynthia.

Detective Kelly had a smirk on his face as he pulled up. He approached Cynthia and quickly replied "You can stop the ass kissing officer Brown. I will meet you at the station. I do not want anyone to talk to the driver until I arrive and do not let her out of your sight. I will call you once I am done with the scene interrogation I am doing now. Do you understand?"

"Loud and clear sir. See you at the police station." Replied Cynthia. It was strange; their conversation was more like a drill sergeant had been interrogating her rather than a senior detective barking orders.

*****

Cynthia Brown arrived at the police station several minutes before Detective Kelly. She escorted Arrferria Carson into booking. Arrferria was now completely frozen by the ordeal and had stopped her protests. Once Cynthia filed all the necessary paperwork, she placed Arrferria into the interrogation room as ordered by Detective Kelly. Cynthia had put it in as a routine stop where the speeder was being 'insubordinate.' However, she followed Detective Kelly's request not to turn in the drugs found at the traffic stop. Something inside her knew that not following the procedure of turning in illegal drug evidence just did not feel right. It was the confidence and the surety with which the detective had spoken as if this were usual for him and that irked Cynthia. However, for now she would be a fly on the wall and observe until this situation made more sense to her.

Detective Kelly arrived at the precinct and walked directly into the interrogation room, bypassing the evidence locker. Although Officer Brown noticed his actions, she pretended not to. He quickly asked Officer Brown to step out of the room while he talked to Arrferria alone.

"Mrs. Arrferria Carson, can you explain to me why you had over eight hundred pills of Oxycodone and Percocet in your possession?" he asked as he entered the room.

Arrferria was crying. "Look, I cannot go to jail." She said in between tears, her sobbing forcing her to voice to break every now and then. "I have a family and a fantastic job. What can I do to make all this shit just…just go away?"

Detective Kelly smirked. "You can start by telling me who you work for and to whom you were going drop off the pills," he said as he pulled out a few pills in an evidence bag, unmarked and unfiled. "I know you are not just some common street peddlers, selling these on corners to whomever comes by."

"You must assure me that I will not go to jail before I start talking. When can I call my lawyer?" Arrferria asked as she sobbed.

"You can call your lawyer when I fucking tell you that it's okay for you to do so," said Detective Kelly as he threw the pills with the evidence bag on the interrogation table. "However, you are going to tell me all I need to know and maybe I will cut you a deal," he told her.

"Okay." Arrferria said, her tears slightly receding. "But you must protect me. I need to know if my family is going to be okay. I do not want to lose my job at the hospital."

Detective Kelly raised his eyebrows, as if surprised. "So, you work at the hospital? Which one? What is your job there?"

"I am the Director of a pharmacy." Arrferria replied.

A smile broke out from the corner of the detective's mouth. "So, you are stealing opioids from your job? That is ingenious." He leaned back. "You got a free supply of drugs. I mean, you must be the ringleader of your operation. I am sorry but I will not be able to help you. This looks like RICO charges for you, Arrferria." He smiled, looking directly at her. He knew she was not a leader; not at all.

Arrferria was herself surprised and got confused. "Wow, I…uhm…I am no damn ringleader or drug kingpin. Why are you going to charge me with RICO charges?!" Her voice was rising now. "I am just a small piece of the operation. Angelita Dallas is who you want!" Tears were coming back now. "Just…just cut a deal with me and I will tell you everything I know. I cannot go to prison! I have kids that need me!"

Detective Kelly knew he had her. "I think you can use the phone now. You are going to need your lawyer here to help you out of…this. Let me know when you are ready for the deal," Detective Kelly said as he got up, leaving a crying Arrferria in the chair alone.

*****

This arrest before had been a remarkably successful coincidence. The detective just hoped that the officer Cynthia Brown would not pry her nose where it did not belong. Goody-good police officers like her had a habit of putting operations like his in jeopardy.

The detective got the details of the hospital that Arrferria was working in and noted that it was not too large of a pharmacy to even be the central location of such an operation. He knew that there was more information about this drug operation. Even if someone altered the missing drugs documents at the hospital, there was no way Arrferria could steal over hundreds of pills without being noticed. There had to be more hospitals involved, Detective Kelly thought. He continued to listen to Arrferria as she explained the entire drug organization operation. Detective Kelly knew that this new drug game player would need someone deep in the "belly of the beast;" someone with authority. He would help them… for a fee of course.

The detective arrived at Angelita Dallas's hospital early that morning. He witnessed Angelita getting out of her car to enter the hospital. As she locked her car door Detective Kelly came up to her and called her name. Angelita turned around in a flash, shocked at the sudden appearance of the man. It took her a moment to register that he was showing her his badge.

"Angelita Dallas, I need to talk to you in private." Detective Kelly said as he put his badge back in his pocket.

Angelita straightened herself. "How can I help you officer?"

"Do you know Arrferria Carson?" he asked.

Angelita took a moment to respond, feigning still being confused and shocked at his sudden appearance. The detective noticed a glint of shock in her face, of sudden realization.

"That name does ring a bell. I am not sure I know her. What is the problem?" she asked.

The detective laughed. "That's funny because she knows you." He crossed his arms. "She was caught with a large amount of prescription pills and Arrferria named you as her boss. In fact, I was informed of an entire drug organization made up of hospital pharmacy directors stealing and selling Oxycodone and Percocet pills all over the tri-state area. Now, are you sure you do not know Arrferria Carson?"

Angelita was starting to breath heavily. "I have no idea what you are talking about, Officer." She was starting to sweat. "Am I under arrest? Do I need to call my attorney?"

The detective smiled. "No, you are not under arrest for now. I am just giving you a courtesy conversation. I am just letting you know that sometimes police protection can be a good thing." He reached inside his jacket, pulling out a card. "Now here is my business card. Please call me if you happen to remember Mrs. Carson. However, my invitation for protection has a time limit. You have 24 hours to decide. After that, our next meeting will be conducted a lot differently. Do you understand?"

Angelita swallowed. She knew this was not a courtesy offer for protection. "I understand perfectly, Officer. Now have a wonderful day." Angelita said, taking hold of the card and staring at it as the detective exited.

As Detective Kelly walked back to his undercover vehicle, Angelita looked at him, not moving from the parking lot. She waited until he exited the hospital property and immediately started to plan her escape from the area. In her head, she had wondered why Arrferria did not drop off the pills last night to Lisa Chin.

Angelita quickly called her boss and explained she was feeling nauseous. Her boss instructed her to go home, and she did as fast as she could. Angelita had to remove the remaining pills from her house. She had money saved and would have to use it immediately. She wanted to avoid issues at her workplace. Angelita decided to submit her job resignation by email, too. The detective gave her 24 hours to decide. However, she would only need ten to leave the city and the country. There was no way she was going to work for the police.

Chapter 10
Asking Too Many Questions

Bootsy was making another one of his usual drug deliveries. This time, though, the delivery was for the Richard Kelly drug organization. He was there early in the morning before the sun was even up.

Bootsy had no loyalty to either Sandy Lopez or Richard Kelly's organizations and delivered drugs to both regularly. It was strictly business, and he knew from experience that being aligned with either organization exclusively would be bad for business. It was far too profitable to be the go-to, trusted delivery guy for both.

So, Bootsy remained neutral and kept his business endeavors close to his vest. The only other person who knew about his dealings was Sophia Fire. She was someone to whom he entrusted his secrets. Sophia herself was Jamaican born, a woman who preferred practicality over anything else. She was not one to flaunt her beauty, even though she had it in droves. She kept her head clean shaved. She was Bootsy's enforcer and closest confidante.

She was certainly beautiful, and she used that attribute along with her knowledge of the drug game to assist Bootsy. Her loyalty to him was something that would never have been questioned and she always ensured that Bootsy was never disrespected. Their alliance though was a secret to most because people rarely ever saw them together. Still, for those who knew, it was safe to assume that if Bootsy was at any location, Sophia Fire was not too far from him, always watching.

As Bootsy drove his tractor trailer hauling new vehicles into the rear parking lot of the dealership, Sal Antonio flagged him to park the tractor trailer to a marked location to unload the vehicles. Sal Antonio worked for Richard Kelly and managed all the security and enforcement for Richard's drug organization. To Richard, Sal was not the smartest or brightest in his organization, but what he lacked in intelligence, Sal made up with his loyalty. He was relentless when it came to anything related to Richard Kelly's interest. His Italian heritage and sense of pride made him a formidable man to deal with due to his excellent knowledge of security. Sal knew how to size up a person and to dispose of them should Richard ever need it done. Richard had first encountered Sal Antonio when he was a young teen. He had noticed that Sal was homeless, and he provided Sal with his first job opportunities. Although Richard constantly tested Sal's loyalty in their initial years, at this point there was no question that Sal would take a bullet or go to prison for Richard Kelly without a second thought.

Bootsy watched as Sal Antonio ordered his workers to remove all the vehicles from his trailer carrier. It was interesting to him that Richard's drug organization chose to hide their narcotics in the front and rear bumpers of all the new vehicles. Since there were no reason to hide the smell that so very clearly produced from the drugs. Bootsy had seen dealers in the past use mustard to disguise the smell from K9s and even other animals who would be keen to sniff out the goods. Yes, it would be strange to see mustard covered packages coming out of a brand-new car, (but it certainly was worth it to fool any drug sniffing animals). It was obvious to Bootsy that this drug organization had no fear of police involvement. Therefore, he realized that Richard Kelly's drug organization had the local police on his payroll.

Always wearing a hoody, Bootsy was consistent with his attire when he did any drug transport and today, he was in his usual all black attire. Bootsy stepped out of his truck and walked towards Sal Antonio. The men greeted each other and walked to inspect all the new vehicles to ensure that all vehicles were in good condition. If everything were good Bootsy would receive his payment from Sal.

Bootsy started his usual cheerful conversation.

"What is going on with my Italian stallion friend? It is another beautiful morning, don't you agree? How was your weekend, brother Sal?" Bootsy asked. Sal who had a serious look about him, too serious to match Bootsy's own, happy-go-luck vibes.

"It was okay, big man." Sal answered in a flat tone. "Just stand near your truck until we are finished checking each vehicle. Then you will get paid," Sal answered. "Hurry up men! I want all these vehicles checked and put back together for sale in 45 minutes tops. Does everyone understand?" Sal asked.

Bootsy saluted Sal, as if impressed with his assertiveness. "Damn, I do not work for you, but I understand!" Bootsy said, laughing. "Now, recently you are calling me big man brother Sal. If you have not noticed, I have lost over seventy-five pounds since our last visit. From now on you can call middle-aged, slim, and sexy! Wait until our next visit. I am going to have six pack abdominal muscles and everything. These foreign bitches' better lookout for me. I am going to be an international pimp with my google translator mobile application ready. No bitch is going to be safe from my sexy ass."

Sal smiled to himself this time. "If you do not get your ass next to your truck now, there will not be another visit here for you. Now, no more jokes Mr. Middle Aged, Slim, and Sexy. We should be done here soon. If everything is copesthetic you will be paid soon, capiche?"

"Wow, after all these drop-offs I have done for you folks, now you want to threaten me like that. Okay brother Sal, you are running the show. I will just listen to my music on my headphones until you folks are finished." Bootsy replied in his usual demeanor.

Unbeknownst to Sal, Bootsy was again in constant communication with Sophia Fire. Bootsy with his hoodie pulled over his head watched Sal's men reassemble the new vehicles bumpers back and drive each to their designated parking spaces.

He began to talk to Sophia in his earpiece.

"Sophia, how is everything looking from your location? These motherfuckers are taking all day to finish this delivery." Bootsy spoke, whispering slightly.

Sophia's voice came in the earpiece. "Everything is cool, mon. I got my eyes on Sal Antonio. That blood clot makes me angry. Why he called you big man when it is clear by just seeing you that you have a slim figure now. You achieved massive weight loss."

"Right and thank you for noticing my weight journey gains," Bootsy replied. "That motherfucker is not noticing a brother's positive gains. Hell, I am working hard to get sexy for these young bitches. However, just continue to watch my back until I am long gone. This will be our only delivery for today. I will meet you at our spot later today. I got to try using my new translation mobile app on this woman I met online from Honduras. You know, she doesn't speak a lick of English and all my Spanish words come from the Taco Bell menu. Oh, and the inappropriate words I learned from Jesus in the fifth grade! Puta pendejo (asshole whore)!" He laughed heartily as he said it. "So, this mobile app is going to help me in getting that fat Honduran ass tonight!"

Sophia laughed heartily too. "Boy, are you really using a translation app to pick up women?!"

It took a while until Bootsy started laughing with her.

"I thought you were fucking joking when you told Sandy Lopez that shit. Wow, let me know how it turns out for you. Now, let me focus on these motherfucking skunks."

Both were chuckling before Bootsy suddenly heard Sophia's very urgent voice in the earpiece. "Hold up, two vehicles are entering the main parking lot of the car dealership. It looks like Richard Kelly in one car and a Black woman in the other car."

"Okay. Bootsy replied. "These guys here are finishing now. Sal Antonio is walking towards me with the payment. I will talk to you later."

Sal Antonio walked towards Bootsy with a large duffle bag. It made a satisfyingly heavy thudding sound as Sal dropped it on the ground. Bootsy opened the bag quickly and checked the money inside. Everything was there.

Bootsy wasted no time giving Sal a handshake and getting back to his tractor trailer. He had a smile on his face while driving out of the parking lot of the car dealership.

Sal, however, was very visibly upset. He had wanted to get this delivery done well before Richard Kelly even arrived at his car dealership. A lack of efficiency would not be a good look for him as a close confidant of Richard Kelly. Sal knew the Richard Kelly would notice if it took too long to deliver and unload the drugs, it meant that more could go wrong.

Sal understood Richard Kelly would not be happy with the time it took to remove the drugs and park the new vehicles. It was understood by both men that Richard Kelly could never be seen at any drug deal. "Plausible deniability, you see." Richard Kelly had told Sal many years ago. "If I'm not there, the authorities made a drug bust they would just chalk it up to a few bad apples taking advantage of their position at my car dealership," explained Richard.

Richard Kelly was the head of the drug organization; without him no one would make any money. It was Richard's name and contacts that moved the product, not the product itself. It was a question of reliability and long-term relationships when it came to Richard Kelly. This man liked to keep his friends and enemies close, so that when the time came, he would pit them against each other. The old divide and conquer strategy.

Sal knew this as he walked into the dealership showroom and prepared for Richard Kelly's harsh comments. Both Richard Kelly and Alcia Adams arrived within seconds of each other. Alcia always arrived early at work as she had to put financial reports together for Richard and place them on his desk as soon as he arrived. The sheer amount of creative accounting needing to be done at the car dealership, she had her work cut out for her. Seeing her boss at work sometimes made Alcia grimace. However, that expression was tame compared to the sigh she made when she noticed the delivery of new vehicles to the car dealership. She was not pleased to see these new vehicles being delivered this morning. Alcia knew that the car dealership was not selling many vehicles and now Richard Kelly ordered even more expensive ones at that. This did not make sense to her, and she was determined to inform Richard Kelly of her concerns. Even businesses run as a cover needed to maintain that cover, regardless of who Richard Kelly had in his pocket.

"Good morning, Richard." Alcia Adams spoke to her boss as they both went inside the showroom. "I see we got another delivery of new vehicles. How are we going to justify purchasing these vehicles, if I may ask as your finance officer? I already have the car manufacturer asking for payment. All these vehicles are on consignment from them. We had six months to make our payment and those payments were due two months ago. I will need your help to make this make sense," said Alcia.

Richard Kelly had stopped when she had greeted him and listened to her politely with a smirk on his face as usual. "Good morning to you too, Alcia." he said, straightening his belt. "You can make the past due payments to the manufacturer today in full. Also, we will need to schedule another marketing campaign to sell these new vehicles. It is going to be spectacularly huge," said Richard Kelly as he looked around the dealership. He was blissfully ignoring his accountant's upset face. "I want this car dealership swarming with customers this weekend. Alcia, please remember you are here to assist me and not to make things difficult. Just make the damn payment to the car manufacturer and leave everything else to me," instructed Richard.

"I...understand," replied Alcia visibly upset. "However, you are not the one who must deal with the IRS audits. It is getting too difficult and nigh impossible to prove where all this cash is coming from even when I do not know most of the time," said Alcia. She wanted to say much more but decided against it when she saw Sal Antonio coming towards them. "Let me get started making the payments. Good morning, Sal," Alcia spoke as she greeted the head of security. In her haste she did not bother to return Sal's extended hand as she blew past him.

Sal came forward to interrupt their conversation and not a moment too soon. Richard Kelly had grown tired of Alcia's constant meddling. Richard directed his confidant (Sal) to his office as they began to converse. As both men enter the office, Richard began to discuss Alcia's future in their organization.

"Sal, why were the vehicles delivered so late this morning? Bootsy is never late. So, what is your excuse?" Richard asked, with a voice that was clearly meant to be accusatory.

Sal Antonio was nervous. He was entrusted with so much of the business and Sal did not want to have let his boss down. "Richard, I was unaware that you ordered so many cars. It would usually take about half an hour, tops, to unload the vehicles," Sal explained. As he continued talking, Richard sighed, as if indicating that he had heard this sort of excuse before. "But this morning it took us about fifteen extra minutes. These new vehicle bumpers are made of plastic and putting them back on without noticeable damage is difficult. I did not want to waste even more money by having to order replacements."

"Fuck those bumpers, Sal!" The man boomed. "If the bumpers are damaged, we will just sell the vehicles as is. See, the problem is solved. In the future, you will move the cars a lot faster or schedule the drop-off earlier. It is that simple, Sal."

Sal had his head down, looking at the floor. "It will not happen again, Sir. However, Bootsy picks the delivery times. Do you want me to take that responsibility away from him? How can I make this issue go away?" asked Sal.

Richard Kelly was not happy with Sal's solution. "Hell no!" Richard yelled. "Let Bootsy continue to schedule the delivery. He is the only one that is dependable in this whole damn organization." Richard sat down as he said it, breathing, trying to calm down. "However, to make me happy again please do me a small favor and get rid of Alcia tonight. She is asking too many questions and I feel if the federal government puts pressure on Alcia, she will cooperate with them to save her own too honest ass. But do it quickly and quietly. It needs to look like an accident."

Sal Antonio took a moment and nodded. This was his chance to win back Richard's trust. "I am on it. You should be looking to replace her in the job immediately," Sal replied.

Richard Kelly laughed. "Oh, do not you worry about that! Alcia might be smart with numbers, but here is something she could never have calculated, and it was right under her nose! She has been training her replacement for the last six months. I am going to promote that sexy blonde junior accountant by Friday. We need to mourn Alcia for a few days before filling her position!" told Richard.

Richard Kelly laughed, and Sal joined in. Sal then put a plan in motion to make the words of defiance against the dealership owner the last ones Alcia Adams would ever say.

*****

Alcia Adams had left the car dealership later that day and was taking a shortcut to her house. It had been a long day, and she was eager to finally get home and relax.

On any other day, she would take her regular route home. Tonight, though, Alcia was already running late, and she knew using the Boyd highway would be like being in a parking lot because of rush hour traffic. Walking would have been faster.

While driving Alcia was playing her music loudly. She wanted to escape from the tense day by playing her favorite song. Her shoulders begging for a massage and her legs were feeling weak as she pushed on the gas pedal to accelerate. As she started to sing to her favorite song not every word came as naturally as it would any other day. The detour she chose to take tonight did not allow her to really focus on the music, either.

Alcia turned into a rural road with few streetlights and large ditches on each side. Considering that this route would take off a half of an hour from her usual route, Alcia was far too focused in looking forward and not behind her. The car behind her was speeding considering the rural road conditions. However. in her current state of mind, Alcia did not notice, at least until the speeding car was directly behind her car and struck it from behind.

Alcia Adams was stunned, dazed, and pressed down hard to the gas pedal in confusion. In any other situation, she would have stepped on the brake and confronted the unknown driver. However, she noticed her surroundings and decided against this confrontation. The unknown speeding car hit her vehicle again and caused Alcia to drive into a large ditch. Alicia took a moment to get her bearings as she moved to open the door, she realized she was trapped. Alcia had fallen in a way that made it impossible for her to get out of her vehicle.

The unknown driver was Sal Antonio and he quickly stepped out of the once speeding car with a handgun. Sal could hear Alcia crying for help as he smiled a devilish smile. His slicked back hair and Italian dressing style made him look like he was on some sort of dance floor as he walked with a smooth rhythm to towards Alcia's car.

As Sal walked next to her damaged vehicle, he saw Alcia struggling to get out. He approached her and pointed his gun and flashlight in her face. Sal wanted her to see the person that was going to be her executioner.

Alcia's injured face came into view as Sal shone a light onto her and she realized that the help she wanted was not here. Not at all. She continued to cry for help and beg for her life, because what else could she do?

Sal shot her several times in the head and upper torso. It was satisfying to him, seeing a person's life taken from them. It would have been more so if he had been able to look in her eyes, but the condition of her face did not really allow that to happen. Still, it was a good kill for Sal, and he congratulated himself for it.

Sal walked back to his car and grabbed a container of gasoline. He poured it over the crashed vehicle and lit a match before throwing it onto the car. In just a few seconds, Alcia's lifeless body was fully engulfed in flames and this accountant would never disturb Richard Kelly's business ever again.

Chapter 11
Cutting Loose Ends

It was not unusual for a body to be found that fast in this small city. However, this morning when it was discovered, a street construction crew were the first to see the gruesome remains of Alcia Adams. It was clear to anyone that this was not an accident and with the recent string of murders the theory of drugs coming into the fold was likely. This incident was not the most subtle execution, nor an accident in the slightest.

It did take time for the news to travel back to the small city, though. The street construction crew were slow to put out proper barriers on the ditches but had the area roped off just before the police forensic team arrived. They could not disturb the evidence.

Thomas Williams had learned of Alcia Adams' severely burnt body and car found on a dirt road just outside of the city limits later that day. Although Thomas was shocked at first by the news of this incident, he quickly gathered his car keys and raced towards the front door. Thomas needed to get ahead with this story, to see if it was related to his own case of the two murders in the Hampton Heights area of the city. The MO was clearly different. However, gangs and drug organizations rarely left calling cards unless it was for competition.

As Thomas locked the door behind himself and rushed down the stairwell, he bumped into a person by accident. Thomas did not look at the man's face and in his hurry decided not to. He just simply apologized to the unidentified man for the innocent encounter and began to rush past him. However, the man was upset, as he raised his arms and began to curse at Thomas. The man insisted on a more sincere apology from him.

Thomas ignored the man's suggestion and continued walking down the steps towards the street where his vehicle would be parked. The man was insistent. "I told you, I'm sorry." Thomas said.

"I know you are not walking away while I am fucking talking to you. I said that your apology was not good enough. Now try it again and this time with fucking feeling bitch," said the unidentified man.

Thomas had dealt with difficult neighbors before. However, to be so rude at merely a bump had him seething. Thomas was not going to have any of it. He wanted to just get to his car and leave, damn this man and his demands. "Are you fucking kidding me? That is the best apology you are going to get from me, my friend! Who the fuck are you?" asked Thomas.

As Thomas said the words, the unidentified man pulled out a handgun from his jacket and pointed it towards the reporter. "I bet you wished you gave me that fucking apology now you little bitch," spoke the unidentified man.

Thomas Williams froze. His eyes could only focus on the gun and not the face of the man. Even his voice was breaking. Thomas was scared. "Come on man. All of this for an innocent bump on the stairwell." Thomas said, before taking a breath and trying to resolve the situation. "You need to just put down the gun and we both just walk away from this incident like it never happened. Are you from around here? I have never seen you in this apartment complex before. Whoa man, please! Put down the gun," begged Thomas.

The unidentified man smiled. "Same ole Thomas Williams, always asking fucking questions."

Thomas was puzzled. Was it a stalker? A criminal he convicted throughout his career. Why had this man just called him by his name? thought Thomas.

"How do you know my name? Again, who are you? Who told you where I lived? Just put down the gun!" demanded Thomas.

Thomas Williams never got an answer and never even got to express the immense shock his body felt before it succumbed to death. The unidentified man fired several shots into Thomas Williams' torso. However, it took a while before Thomas could even scream in pain. In a state of shock,

Thomas tried to run after a second or two, whether upstairs or downstairs, he could not tell. Thomas could not even see clearly ahead of him as he stumbled and fumbled his way forward.

The unidentified man quickly caught up with Thomas, with ease. Thomas was then struck by rapid gunfire again as he reached his apartment entrance. Thomas fell onto the sidewalk near the flower path next to the apartment stairwell. Thomas managed to find a solid object on the ground and quickly grabbed it to throw towards the unidentified man. However, he missed hitting the man with a loose brick.

The unidentified man fired his gun again and struck Thomas in the leg while he remained laying on the ground. The unidentified man stood over Thomas Williams' body and delivered two shots into the reporter's skull.

He died instantly.

The man then walked towards the street and returned with a can of gasoline. He poured it over Thomas' freshly murdered body, blood still oozing through Thomas's clothes, red and dirty, making patterns onto the concrete on the sidewalk. There was a smile on the man's face as he watched the flames engulf Thomas' body.

*****

Detective Kelly was now at the Alcia Adams crime scene. Both Alcia's body and her car were discovered burnt to a crisp. Alcia Adam's car was still smoking when he arrived. It was quickly realized by all the police officers present that this was a homicide. However, confirmation would be needed from the county coroner before an official homicide case could be opened by the police department.

As Detective Kelly walked towards the scene, he thought how this could have played out. Technically, a car could fall into a ditch and a fire could be explained. Things like this can happen and have happened in the past. However, this one clearly showed someone was murdered.

Even as Detective Kelly walked, he saw bits of headlights on the ground marked with evidence markers with the rest of the police officers. They had just arrived too and were figuring out how far the crime scene stretched. Kelly saw the bullet casings, the deep footprints of boots that were clearly too fancy for construction workers and the smell of burning meat.

"Listen up!" Detective Kelly bellowed, and the officers looked at him. "I need this area, 100 yards in all directions taped off immediately and let me know when the county coroner arrives," ordered Detective Kelly. "You got it, detective," replied another police officer.

Detective Kelly then begins asking the first officer on scene some questions.

"Were you the first officer on the scene?" asked Detective Kelly. "Yes, I was the first officer one here, detective." A young police officer answered him. "The vehicle was still on fire when I arrived. I managed to use my fire extinguisher from my squad car to put out the remaining flames. That is when I noticed a body also burning inside the vehicle. I have not touched it, but it was clearly mutilated. Parts of the face were missing," detailed the police officer.

"Excellent work," said Detective Kelly as he patted the officer on his shoulder. "The car license plate is still readable. Did you investigate who this car belongs to officer?" asked Kelly.

"Yes sir. The vehicle belongs to a Ms. Alcia Adams." The officer replied.

"Huh." The detective's hairs on his arms stood up. The revelation puzzled him. He knew that Alcia Adams worked for Richard Kelly as his car dealership accountant. It seemed to him that trouble was brewing in Richard's drug organization. It seemed to Detective Kelly that Richard Kelly was now offing his staff and cleaning house. The detective's instincts were telling him that it might be time to find a new drug organization to extort soon.

"Where is her body now? I want to view it before the coroner arrives." Detective Kelly instructed the police officer.

"Please follow me. However, let me warn you that it is not a sight I would want to see too much of." The police officer replied as he began to walk towards a body bag.

They arrived at the body bag, tiny slivers of smoke coming off it. They could smell her burning flesh through the tightly sealed bag. The body bag itself seemed to radiate heat.

"Okay Detective Kelly please get ready to see something horrible." The police officer said as he began to open the zipper.

"Just open the damn body bag. Like I haven't seen dead bodies before." Detective Kelly snarly replied.

The police officer who was distracted by the detective's comments and he accidentally almost damaged evidence as he opens the body bag. Alcia Adams' body was severely burned. However, the most surprising part of the viewing was Alcia's face, or rather, the lack of it. The body was missing a substantial portion of her skull.

"What the fuck!!! This lady is fucked up!" The detective almost yelled as he put his coat jacket up to cover his mouth and nose. "She was killed before the car was set on fire. What did she do to make someone so damn mad?" He asked the police officer as he shrugged, trying his best not to look at the body. "Okay, zip her body back up and inform the dispatch that we are now dealing with a clear homicide," said Detective Kelly.

"Yes detective. I am on it," replied the police officer.

As Detective Kelly walked back to his car, he got a call. Sitting inside, he took out his phone and saw that Cynthia Brown, the officer who had stumbled upon a new drug organization during a routine traffic stop, was calling him.

"Yes? This is Detective Kelly." He spoke.

"Detective, yes, I…uh…it is Cynthia. I mean…Officer Brown, detective. It is…."

"Yes, what is it? Quickly now," demanded Detective Kelly.

"It is Thomas, sir. Thomas Williams. He has been…he has been murdered, sir." Cynthia Brown said, as if the words were difficult to come by. She was clearly upset. "He was murdered at his apartment a short while ago…"

"Wait, Officer Brown." Detective Kelly interjected, clearly excited at this news and doing his absolute best not to show it to the officer through the sound of his voice. He took a breath, cleared his throat, and talked back to the officer in his most concerning voice.

"Officer Brown, please calm down and talk slowly," said Detective Kelly.

"Detective Kelly, I cannot believe someone fucking killed reporter Thomas Williams. That man single handedly lowered the crime in this city years ago. Why would anyone assassinate this man?" Officer Brown said, very clearly upset, but this time not holding back.

Detective Kelly smiled. "Officer Brown, you are acting like that man was a fucking saint! Everyone has Unclean Hands in this city, officer. Now pull yourself together and meet me at the police headquarters when your initial investigation at the crime scene is completed, understood," asked Detective Kelly.

Cynthia Brown tried to compose herself and took a few breaths on the call. "Understood Sir. I will conduct myself in a professional manner." After that she began to mumble. "I'm sorry, it's just that I admired him." Although she soon caught herself and cleared her throat, replying in a clear voice. "Yes, sir, be professional," said Cynthia Brown.

Both hung up their cellphones. However, Cynthia Brown was puzzled why Detective Kelly was not upset by hearing the news of Thomas Williams' death. Not even an ounce of shock from a man who would have been one of the city's greatest allies in fighting crime. Cynthia knew that the two men shared history and the news of Thomas' death should have affected Detective Kelly emotionally in some manner, if not for a friend, for a colleague of sorts, at least. Cynthia was determined to uncover the reason the men's relationship was distant. To say it was weird to her would have been an understatement if there ever was one.

Chapter 12
Follow Instructions

Thomas Williams' death was broadcasted all over the news and people in the local area were very aware now that things in this town-turned-city weren't really going towards a safer trajectory. Lately there has been more talk of people wanting to leave every single day. Although, it wasn't uncommon in this city to have very few newsworthy murders happening each year. However, the news of the city's beloved reporter created shock waves of uncertainty amongst most of the citizens.

For Lil Ricky, though, it was business as usual. He was meeting his 'forbidden' grandfather at the family-owned Chinese restaurant in the heart of the city. The hustle and bustle in that area made it easy for the likes of Lil Ricky to go unnoticed. He made sure to park his car in the alley behind the restaurant to avoid being seen by people like his mother and any enemies he or his grandfather may have because they had plenty.

Lil Ricky and his crew needed firearms and his grandfather (Mr. Chin) had a monopoly on these illegal firearms sales in the surrounding area. It was a territory that his grandfather had carved out for himself years ago during the gang war years. Mr. Chin could now safely export weapons and store them in his restaurant while also conducting his legitimate business operations.

Lil Ricky had grown up hearing horror stories about his grandfather from his mother in the past. He had recently reached out to his grandfather for assistance in acquiring firearms. After their initial encounter, the men started to rekindle their family relationship. It wasn't the typical way to begin a family relationship, sure, however Lil Ricky felt he needed some kind of male guidance in his life. His biological father was murdered 15 years ago when he was only 4 years old. Therefore, to Lil Ricky his grandfather was the closest he had in his bloodline to a father.

Lil Ricky knocked on the rear entrance of the restaurant and was invited in by a server who recognized who he was. He was led through the staff break room area where his grandfather was sitting at his usual table. Mr. Chin immediately got up and greeted Lil Ricky warmly.

"There is my long-lost grandson. At this moment you are fourth on my most favored list, you know. However, you are quickly moving up my list," said Mr. Chin.

Lil Ricky didn't find his grandfather's words amusing and quickly changed the conversation. "Yo, what are you talking about? For all I care you can keep that shit list grandfather. I am here to get some more sticks (guns) for a big job. You got me or not?" Lil Ricky asked. "Like I said, my crew and I are executing something big soon." Lil Ricky felt irritated, and he didn't want to exchange pleasantries. He was there for business only during this visit. 'Isn't that what men do?' Lil Ricky thought to himself.

Mr. Chin kept his smile up and laughed. "I am just fucking with you grandson. You know that you are really in third place. Cheer up, you still have room for improvement. Do you want something to eat? Your new grandmother is making chicken fried rice." asked Mr. Chin.

"Hell, yes, I want some chicken fried rice, some chicken wings and a large side of some fucking guns." Lil Ricky said, rubbing his hands together and licking his lips. "But we got to move quickly. I know mom is going to call me soon. That woman always senses when I am fucking up," explained Lil Ricky.

Mr. Chin's smile quickly faded. Not out of anger or anything, but from a look of concern. "Please let your mother know that we have been dealing with each other for over a year now. She just started talking to me recently and I do not want to lose her again," begged Mr. Chin.

Lil Ricky was puzzled. He was unaware that his grandfather and mother had a relationship like that at all. Mr. Chin continued. "I was a real asshole to her when you were younger. However, I only behaved that way because she was fucking with your dumb ass daddy. Of all the Black men in this country ass city that she could have picked, my daughter chose a low-life conman and drug dealer. However, something good did come out of their relationship and that was you. Of all my grandchildren, you are the only one not a punk bitch. The others are college graduates but have no street sense and, in this world, you need both." Mr. Chin told his now confused grandson, who was munching on a few items the restaurant servers had bought them.

"Now Lil Ricky you have a sharp street sense like me. However, I am waiting to see if you are as intelligent as your mother always brags about to me. Are you still in school?" asked Mr. Chin.

Lil Ricky's confusion turned to laughter. "Did you just insult and praise me at the same damn time?" asked Lil Ricky. "Mom doesn't know shit about me coming over here to visit you. Can you just show me the guns so I can get the fuck out of here? I need some automatic weapons too, real Scarface type shit," demanded Lil Ricky.

Mr. Chin sighed. He knew he wasn't getting through to his grandson; not yet. His grandfather knew that Lil Ricky needed to become a man before he could understand the importance of being an educated gangster. Getting involved with the wrong people required a level head and a sharp sense of self-preservation; his grandson lacked both in equal measure.

"Okay, follow me into my office; we can talk in there." Mr. Chin said, wiping his face with a napkin as he got up.

Both were in Mr. Chin's office for over an hour arguing over the price of the guns and ammunition. Finally, they agreed, and Lil Ricky began to load the firearms into his new minivan that he recently purchased from Richard Kelly's car dealership. It would have been obvious that a blacked-out van behind a restaurant loading anything at all would look suspicious. However, neither were particularly worried. Unfortunately, they should have been.

Unbeknownst to both men, Lisa Chin had arrived early to her meeting with her father. She quickly noticed her son carrying large boxes out of the restaurant rear entrance and placing them into his new vehicle. Furious at the sight of her son dealing with her father behind her back, Lisa intuitively knew that she had to do something about it.

However, she regained her composure and waited patiently to see just how her son and father's newly discovered relationship had blossomed. She continued to observe the two men as each assisted the other in packing Lil Ricky's vehicle. Once their task was completed, both hugged each other and went separate ways.

Little Ricky never really thought about the many consequences of his actions. He never really understood why his mother had told him to stay away from the only family male figure in his life. Lisa Chin rarely mentioned her father to him at all in a positive manner. Lisa Chin knew that her son should never trust her father because Mr. Chin only cared about money. That hard lesson she had learned 15 years ago.

Lisa Chin pondered for a while after Lil Ricky left the alley behind her father's restaurant. There were so many ways to try to make sense of what she just witnessed she thought as she began running over each scenario in her head. Lisa decided not to meet her father today. Instead, she quickly left the alley and followed her son for a short distance until he reached his friend's house. Lisa observed the young men unload boxes of unknown merchandise.

Lil Ricky and his friend clandestinely moved the large boxes out of their mini-van and into a small house. Lisa Chin knew that if her father was involved then guns were also a part of the deal. She could not believe Lil Ricky was this stupid to deal with illegal firearms and then even dumber to get the weapons from her father. Lisa grows more upset at the thought of her father involving her son in everything illegal. She knew that Lil Ricky wanted a male figure in his life but not from her sorry ass father she thought.

She had made a conscious effort in the past not to bring strange men around her son. Lisa even dated some men that others may have considered to be excellent candidates for marriage. However, none of them were worthy enough to meet her son; let alone worthy enough to be a prominent figure in Lil Ricky's life. Lisa had now decided that she had all the information she needed to conclude that her father was up to no good and she must save her son from the fate that had been inflicted on his father had been inflicted on 15 years ago.

Chapter 13

Poetic Justice

Angelita Dallas was dismayed by her friend's betrayal. Detective Kelly knew about her entire drug organization, and he had given her an ultimatum that she could not refuse. Angelita knew that her best option was to leave the country immediately.

After she had submitted her job resignation by email that morning, she placed her cellphone in silent mode. Angelita could not be distracted by her boss asking why she decided to quit her job with such short notice. She knew she'd be getting a flurry of emails, calls, messages and even a surprise visit to her home soon, out of concern, anger, or just pure curiosity from others.

Angelita knew why she needed to hurry. She went into the top drawer of her small safe she kept in her closet. Inside she kept all her real jewelry, her registered concealed weapon and all her important papers including her birth certificate, deed to her home and passport. Her weapon of choice was something she didn't really look at with satisfaction as she stared but for a moment at the hot pink twenty-two caliber gun. Still, she quickly picked it up, packed it with the rest of the stuff and was on her way.

Next, Angelita went to her bank to withdraw nine thousand dollars from her account for travel money and the rest of her checking and saving accounts funds were wire transferred to her bank in the Bahamas. She made sure to withdraw only nine thousand dollars to avoid security check problems at the airport. Angelita knew that carrying more than ten thousand dollars while traveling in the United States would require filling out additional forms by the customs officials and that situation had to be avoided at all costs.

Angelita returned home and she rapidly packed three large bags with hidden compartments that she used to hide the money she had just taken out of the bank. She also kept sizeable amounts of funds in her house for 'just in case' instances like this one. Overall, she had over two hundred thousand dollars now stored in her luggage with her clothing. It wasn't the best way to hide the money, but it was the best she could do on such short notice.

Each second that passed, Angelita grew more concerned and more suspicious. She looked outside her home's window to see if anyone unfamiliar was parked outside. Angelita couldn't be too obvious, either. Once she determined that her neighborhood was safe from any unwanted eyes, she rushed to place her luggage into her car.

She turned on her car ignition and started to drive out of her driveway when Angelita looked in her rear mirror, she noticed several police cars speeding in her direction. Angelita pressed her car pedal hard and tried to speed away from the police. However, before she could make a turn onto the street that led out of her neighborhood. Her car was struck by an oncoming vehicle.

Not wearing her seat belt while driving, Angelita was ejected from her vehicle. She landed on the pavement along with bits of glass from the car's windshield and pieces of the car. Her great escape plan was over.

*****

High pitch sounds engulfed her ears from sirens as a few figures tried to talk to her. It took her a while to come back to her senses before she was able to realize what had happened. A high-pitched ringing sound was still in her ears, not letting her concentrate on what anyone was saying to her.

Angelita Dallas had received a moderate number of injuries from the car crush. However, she would survive. In a daze, Angelita quickly rose to her feet, but she was informed to lay down until help arrived. The paramedics arrived on the scene and placed Angelita on a medical stretcher. She was stunned and confused. Her head was thumping, and she developed a severe headache that seemed to take over her whole body. However, before the medics could put Angelita in the ambulance, a police officer arrived. The paramedics stopped in their tracks as they saw the officer motioning them to stop as he reached into his jacket and pulled out his badge.

It was a certain detective that had arrived and despite the protests of the paramedics, he was taking over the situation. Detective Kelly smiled as he read Angelita's Miranda rights to her, not a sliver of concern on his face at the woman who was bleeding and concussed.

"You have the right to remain silent. Anything you say can and will be used against you in a court of law. You have the right to an attorney. If you cannot afford an attorney, one will be provided for you. Do you understand the rights I have just spoken to you? With these rights in mind, do you wish to speak to me?"

Angelita could barely put the words together, let alone realize who had just come up to her. In her mind, it was still a puzzle that was yet to be solved. "What? Who are you? I need to go to the hospital. Please!" She said, looking confused and bewildered.

Detective Kelly grinned. "Oh, you are going to the hospital and then to jail." He said, as he pointed to the paramedics, who loaded the woman onto the back of the ambulance. The detective entering the ambulance right behind the stretcher. Detective Kelly cuffed Angelita to the stretcher. He also left his car at the accident scene and had decided to accompany the paramedics and Angelita to the hospital.

The detective had ordered both paramedics to the front of the ambulance. While one paramedic was driving the other contacted the hospital. However, he had a look of concern for Angelita, and he was constantly looking at the detective's interaction with her.

"We have been following you all day." Detective Kelly said to Angelita, who was slowly realizing her position and her situation. Even in her current state, she was becoming visibly nervous by the second. "We know about the wire transfer of funds, and we found a large amount of money in your luggage.

You are one stupid black bitch. All you had to do was pay for protection and your organization would have still been running smoothly. However, that option is now voided. Angelita Dallas you will be charged with the Racketeering Influenced and Corrupt Organizations Act."

Angelita started to cry both out of pain and out of dejection. "A RICO charge for me? I am not a big kingpin drug dealer. I work five days a week. Please do not charge me. This is my first offense. I have never been in trouble before. Can you show some mercy detective? I was scared, that's the only reason I tried to leave. Please listen to me," plead Angelita.

The detective laughed. "Girl, you are looking at twenty years in prison minimally and a fine of $250,000 dollars. We will not be cutting any deals with you either. I am going to make an example out of you bitch! You people are forgetting who really runs this damn city. After you, every black, brown, and yellow person in this city will understand that they must pay a fee to do business here."

Angelita didn't have the energy nor the guile at that moment to retort back. Her head was still thumping, hard. "Can we work something out detective? I am not built for prison life. What can I do to fix this problem? Just name it. I will do anything you ask and more!" Angelita said as she sobbed.

"Oh, now, now listen to Ms. Uppity Educated and Fancy nigger bitch!" Detective Kelly said in a deep voice. "You are barking up the wrong tree. I like my women pale with big tits and no ass and your black ass don't fit the description. There is just too much dragging in your wagon for me! There are no more moves left for you to play. Now I hope those cuffs fit you nicely while you're lying on that stretcher," stated Detective Kelly.

Finally, the ambulance stopped. They had arrived at the hospital.

*****

Angelita Dallas was handcuffed in her hospital bed for two weeks as she healed from her wounds. She used this time to establish and defend her criminal case with her lawyer. Angelita's lawyer tried several times to get her a plea deal. However, no deal was made.

Eventually, Angelita's trial was on the local news and surrounding areas daily. Knowledge of her drug organization was now common knowledge to all. Each one of her drug organization members testified against her for lesser sentences. Angelita now realized that she would have to face the RICO charges alone.

It only took a jury of her peers three days to deliberate and make their decision. Although the drugs she sold were not large kilos of cocaine or heroin, the fact that Oxycodone and Percocet pills were legal and sold to children held just as much weight in the jurors opinion. Angelita Dallas was sentenced to twenty-five years to life for her role in the drug organization.

Once Angelita was transferred from jail to federal prison, she realized the severity of her situation. Her world as she knew it was over. No longer could she go on lavish vacations, wear expensive clothes, eat at expensive restaurants, or feel the touch of a man. The female prisoners there were cunning and vicious. Trouble started for Angelita on her second night at the facility. Two large women approached her asking for a cigarette.

"Hi pretty bitch. Does your fine ass have a cigarette?" the first one said, striding towards her, not stopping as Angelita started to back away.

"Do not talk to my new bitch like that, Amelia." The second woman, just as large, interrupted her. "You know I always keep a pretty bitch by my side. My last bitch got parole and now I am in search of someone to take her place. Look at her. Her skin is all soft looking. I can tell she moisturizes on the regular. Pretty face, thick waist. I think this little redbone bitch will do fine."

Angelita was used to being the boss. Used to having her way. Even in prison, she had yet to let go of her pride. "I do not have any fucking cigarettes. Now leave me the fuck alone!" she shouted.

"Who does this bitch think she is talking to?" The first one asked the other, smiling. "Bitch, bring your ass on here now and give me some sugar! I want to taste the lips that are quick to talk shit to me. Now come here!"

The large woman grabbed Angelita by her hair and punched her in the face. The other large woman started kicking Angelita in the face and stomach. Angelita screamed for help. However, no one came to her rescue. Other inmates watched in awe as the large women beat Angelita unconscious. Correctional officers eventually stopped the attack. However, Angelita needed immediate medical attention. The two large women were placed in solitary confinement for three months for their role in their deadly and almost fatal attack on a fellow inmate.

While on the medical ward, Angelita was prescribed Oxycodone for pain. She quickly realized that it was easier to cope with prison life if she was intoxicated. The same pills she once sold were the ones used to ease her pain. Funny, wasn't it?

Weeks went by and Angelita had healed bruises on her torso and two small scars on her face. One on the left side of her jaw and the other to the crease of her right eyelid. Once she was fully healed from her wounds. Angelita was allowed into the general population again with the other prisoners. She stayed to herself mostly to avoid any new physical attacks.

Angelita was not happy about what happened to her face at all. In her mind she did not understand what she said or did to provoke those two big bitches to attack her.

Her first days back in the general population weren't so bad. However, within days the two large women were back in general population as well. The two quickly noticed Angelita to be alone. So, they walked coordinated towards her location.

"There's my baby. Hey there pretty lips." The second of the two had spoken first this time. "Girl I was thinking about you the entire time I was in solitary confinement. Just the thought of you eating my pussy kept me awake all night. I couldn't wait to get out to see your face boo! Just talking about what you are going to do for me makes me tingle down there. OH shit! Now my wet dreams will become reality."

"Hold up, I dreamed about that pretty bitch too." The first one answered back. "I want some of that pussy for myself. Come on now. You got to share. Those juicy lips look like they can satisfy both of us. Can't they pretty lips?" asked the large woman.

Angelita Dallas was prepared this time for the large women attack and quickly pulled out a homemade weapon. When the time came, she swiftly reacted. She lunged forward and cut one of the large women in the face and tried to stab the other with one continuous motion. However, the second large woman dodged her attack and quickly had Angelita in a chokehold. Unable to breathe, Angelita dropped her homemade knife, and she was quickly dragged into a janitor's closet where the inmates stored all the cleaning supplies. Again, there were no guards around to witness this encounter.

One of the large women held her down while the other gagged her mouth closed with a dirty hand towel taken from a rag bucket in the closet. The woman pulled down her pants and sodomized her with a mop handle. Angelita squealed in agony while this act of violence was happening. Once the women were done, they threw a bottle of Oxycodone towards Angelita and left the janitor's closet.

Angelita cried in agony while balled up in a fetal position from the assault. She passed out momentarily and awoke from the pain within seconds. Not knowing where they came from, she grabbed the bottle, and she swallowed three pills to numb her pain. She even thought about overdosing.

It was ironic that the same drugs that she sold to others for a profit is now her only means of escaping her harsh new reality. Angelita had twenty-four more years of this torture to go. If only she could cut a deal with somebody before her demise. She felt defeated knowing that this was not going to end any time soon. Angelita had built a house on sand, and now that house had crumbled.

Chapter 14
Blood Don't Make You Family

AJ Black was leaving his office located at the rear of his barbershop. He used the business to launder money for Sandy Lopez's drug organization. While leaving he noticed a parked car flashing its headlights to get his attention. He walked towards the vehicle irritated at the thought of the FBI meeting him at his place of work in broad daylight. AJ made sure to look in all directions for potential onlookers before he proceeded to enter the federal agents' car. He tried to play it cool, as if he weren't meeting them as an informant.

Once in the car, FBI agents informed AJ that he would need to testify against Sandy Lopez's drug organization. The agents had orders to take him to an undisclosed location while arrest warrants were being served to individual members of his uncle's organization.

Arrest warrants were now issued quickly after the arrest and demise of Angelita Dallas. It usually took years of informant work to even make a dent in major drug cases. However, it only took a few months to convict her. Between the amount of inefficiently hidden information, papers, and everything else they found in Angelita's belongings, it was much easier to request and receive arrest warrants for other drug organizations now.

AJ Black was terrified of the news giving by the FBI agents. However, he knew that this day would eventually arrive. He was nervous about meeting the agents at his workplace, but luckily, they chosen a location he thought was away from prying eyes.

"Shit, is it going down today? I am prepared to testify against anyone involved in Uncle Sandy's organization if you keep your word and not charge my mother and I with any crime. I also need to drive my car out of this parking lot. It would look weird if my car were parked in this parking lot overnight," said AJ.

The FBI agent in the passenger seat looked back at AJ. "Look here you little slick talking piece of shit. You will do what you are told. We are leaving now with you and your fucking car stays here. Do you understand AJ?" explained the agent.

The second agent, the driver, chimed in. "And as far as your mother is concerned. She better start answering her damn cellphone. We have been calling her all morning, but the call is being directed to her voice mail."

AJ Black looked at both before interjecting. "My mother is not going to answer any phone call from a no ID phone number. Please just go to her house and arrest her there. I can explain our arrangement to her once she is safe with me."

"Okay, we can do it your way AJ." The agent in the passenger seat spoke. "However, our top priority is to get you to our safe house immediately. We plan to serve arrest warrants within hours from now."

As the men pulled out of the barbershop parking lot towards their safe house location, in their haste to get things done they hadn't realized they were being watched. One of the barbers had come out of the barbershop for a cigarette break and had seen AJ leave with the FBI agents. He even noticed AJ's car still parked in the parking lot. The barber quickly pulled out his phone and dialed his contact in Sandy Lopez's organization and he informed him about this occurrence.

To say Sandy Lopez was furious would be an understatement. After being informed of his nephew's meeting with the FBI he didn't just feel betrayed, he felt disrespected. The contact had informed the barber to leave the barbershop immediately and follow the FBI agent's car. The barber jumped in his car and followed. He provides Sandy Lopez with information while pursuing the agents.

Sandy Lopez started destroying his mobile home as he thought about his nephew's betrayal and the consequences of his actions towards his organization. His rage could not be hidden from others. The news of AJ Black's working with the federal government was blindsiding. Sandy saw red. The time for planning a subtle solution was over. He wanted to eliminate AJ, now.

Sandy gathered his men into his double wide mobile home to inform them of his exodus plan. He also called his sister to inform her of AJ's cooperating with the FBI to destroy their family's drug organization.

"Maria, can you believe that your half black ass son has turned against his own family?" Sandy said before even acknowledging that it was her picking up the phone. "I begged you not to fuck with them people, but you did it anyway. Now we must shut down our entire operation today. Do you have any fucking idea whose money we are fucking up if our drugs are not sold on schedule? This will cost us everything and we have your stupid ass son to blame. His actions cannot be overlooked this time. Family or not. He must be dealt with," barked Sandy.

Maria Lopez started to cry as she heard all that. Her voice was pleading, and she was bawling by the time she could even get any words out. "Please do not kill my son, hermano (brother)! Your information is wrong. Mentiras (Lies). AJ is a good boy. Sometimes he just likes to boast; that is all. He would never do anything to fuck up what we have going on. He's not that type of kid. He's loyal. He's our blood Sandy," pleaded Maria.

Sandy never considered her words. "I know he's half my blood. It's his other side that fucked up hermana (sister). You know Black people cannot be trusted. Most of them are too damn flashy. They have lived below the poverty line for so long. It seems if they get some money, they must let the whole damn world know about it. That's the fucked-up trait he has Maria."

As he was talking, his phone was blaring up again. The barber following AJ and the FBI agents called Sandy directly. "Espera (Wait), I am receiving another phone call. I want you to remain on hold until I am finished with this incoming phone call. I am not done with you. Dale' (later)."

The barber informed him that AJ went to a location that was known to be a police safe house.

"Mr. Lopez, I have located the safe house. AJ and the FBI just walked into the house. There are no guards posted outside of the house right now. What do you want me to do? Get these motherfuckers?" asked the barber.

Sandy Lopez smiled. "Excellent job. No, not yet. I need you to stay out of sight and let me know if the FBI agents leave AJ alone. I will send my men over shortly. Once they arrive, I want you to join them in eliminating everyone in the house. Do you understand? Compredes (You Understand)?"

"I understand completely." The barber replied. "I will not let them out of my sight."

Once Sandy Lopez's conversation was over with the barber, he informed his sister that he must make another phone call and that it would be wise of her to continue to hold on to the phone until he was ready to talk to her again.

"Maria, are you still there?" Sandy asked her.

"Yes, Sandy please do not kill AJ. He is my only child. Por favor hermano (Please brother)." Maria pleaded.

"Calla te (Be quite)! just hold the fuck on for a few more minutes. I need to make a quick phone call." Sandy said, leaving the woman in tears.

Sandy Lopez called Bootsy and informed him that he must drop off the remaining drugs to his men tonight instead of their normal delivery of every two weeks. He told Bootsy that the transaction will take place at their normal location.

Bootsy was, as anyone would be, puzzled by Sandy's request. However, he agreed and began preparation for tonight's drug delivery immediately.

Sandy ended his call with Bootsy and then ordered his men into his living room for a quick meeting.

"Men, I was just informed that we have a rat in our organization." Sandy spoke as the murmurs of the men talking grew. "My nephew has decided to go against us and help the FBI stop us from feeding our families. This shit is fucked up and I will not tolerate him taking food out of my people's mouth. I need ten men to go to this location where we have a man waiting to show us where the FBI are hiding my nephew. I want the rest of you to get all the money owed to us today. Anyone who does not pay us in full must be put to death. We are shutting down our operation at this location today. By sunrise tomorrow, we must start our journey to Mexico. Now let's go!" yelled Sandy. His men cheered as they start to follow his orders.

Sandy himself realized that his sister was still waiting for him to finish their conversation about AJ. He quickly got back to his phone and resumed the call with his sister as he walked out of the living room, away from his men.

"Maria, are you still there?" He asked but didn't need an answer. Sandy could hear her crying still. "Good. I curse the day that you conceived your son. We can only pray that the cartel shows mercy on us for AJ's treachery. It's out of my hands," informed Sandy.

"Is there anything you can do to avoid them killing him, Sandy?" She pleaded and sobbed, but Sandy interrupted.

"At this point AJ made a decision that would cost him his life. He did it to himself querida (dear)." His voice had gone flat, un-emotional, without empathy.

Sandy Lopez went back to the living room and turned towards his remaining men before ending the phone call with his sister. He wanted Maria to hear his final order to them.

"Men, once everyone is in position and have the necessary firepower and explosive, kill everyone in the safe house. I want no witnesses. I expect this to be done before we leave for Mexico in the morning," Sandy commanded.

He could still hear his sister crying and pleading on the other end of the phone line. However, Maria knew that her cries would be in vain. Sandy had no choice but to kill her son. Maria hung up her phone and began praying to the saints. She went to her bedroom to collect her rosary, put on her grandmother black veil and black clothing to mourn her son as she prepared to leave for Mexico immediately. She came to understand that there was nothing she could do to change her brother's mind.

Chapter 15
Looks Are Deceiving

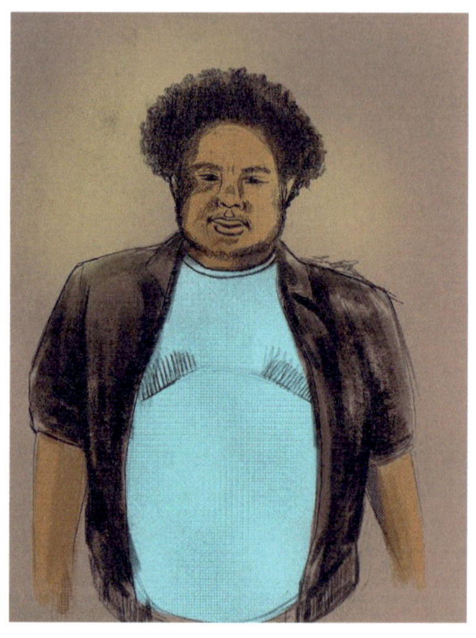

Bootsy arrived at the predetermined location outside of the city to complete the drug drop off for Sandy Lopez as planned. Sophia Fire was in her sniper position observing the scene as the Mexicans started to arrive. It was a little harder to see, the sun had already set. The evening sky was warning of a dark, cloudless night on the horizon. Bootsy exited his tractor trailer to greet the Sandy Lopez's men and lighten the mood with his usual jokes. However, the men were in no mood for his jokes today. They were focused and so was Sophia with her weapon ready to fire at a moment's notice.

"What is going on with my amigos (friends)?" Bootsy exclaimed, smiling his usual smile. "It is not like you folks calling me for an unscheduled delivery. Where is Sandy?" Bootsy started looking around, glancing this way and that, as he said it. "Sandy is normally in attendance for these transactions. Where is he? Is he with one of his sexy ass senoritas (ladies)?" Bootsy was laughing his ass off at this point, with nobody else taking part in it with him. "I know my Spanish is bad. That's the best I can do right now," he said.

Then, one of the Mexican goons that Sandy had employed came up to Bootsy and spoke up. "You talk too fucking much! Fucking Negrito (Blackie)? What the fuck is that? Just stand here and wait until we remove all the products from your trailer." He spoke with a growly tone, before moving back to help with the unloading.

Another Mexican member was shouting orders to the rest. "Let's get this shit quick guys! We need to move all this shit in 30 minutes or less. Jefe (Boss) wants this move to be done as soon as possible." Then he continued to check the inventory to make sure that everything was accounted and paid for as the drugs were unloaded. Despite Sandy's men attitude towards Bootsy, they knew he was reliable. Therefore, they were equally reliable and made sure there were no errors during this transaction.

Bootsy was unfazed by their dispassionate gruntles. "Damn my friend, lighten up a little. I will stand over here as instructed." Bootsy said. He pointed to a location and stood there, as if to make a point. "However, I think your day would go a lot better if you smiled. You folks look constipated with your faces so tight," joked Bootsy.

As he said it, all of Sandy's men that Bootsy could lay his eyes on made a strange face. A few of them even clenched their fists in anger as they continued to unload the drugs from the trailer. They were not at all happy with Bootsy's perpetual happy-go-lucky attitude.

Understanding that this was not the time for anymore jokes, Bootsy decided to simmer down a bit. He mumbled under his breath; a bit angry at their hostile reaction to someone who has been nothing but hospitable despite their unhospitable nature. "I am going to get back into my truck until you folks finish unloading my trailer," Bootsy informed the men. As the men were finishing unloading their product, Bootsy had a bad feeling about this situation. He quickly put in his ear bud and made a furtive phone call to Sophia.

"Sophia, something is not right about this shit." Bootsy's jolly tone had dropped into a more serious, worried one. "I need you to look around and tell me if you see something out of the ordinary. These Mexicans are up to some dirty shit. My left-hand is tingling like a motherfucker. That ain't good!" He said concerned.

"Alright, let me see." Sophia Fire was already monitoring the situation but gave everything a once over. "Where you are sitting everything looks good. The Mexicans are moving the drugs out of the trailer at breakneck speed. However, I just noticed a black minivan parked a block away from you. Whoever is in the minivan is smoking something because a lot of smoke is coming out of the window and it's too much for some cigarettes," she reported.

Bootsy knew that a black minivan was out of place. Whoever was in the vehicle wasn't a bit subtle. It was apparent that a blacked-out van parked in an isolated industrial park at this time of day was there for some superficially shady shit. Anyone glancing at that hulking blacked-out minivan could see it was driven by "wannabe" criminals.

"What? I know it. This feels more like a setup to me. My left-hand tingle doesn't ever do me wrong. It's like my Spidey sense," explained Bootsy.

He tapped on his steering wheel for a bit, before nervously telling Sophia. "Keep an eye on the minivan for now. One of the Mexicans is coming to the driver side of my truck now. They must be finished. I will call you back when I get out of here."

"Okay, I can see everything from my position." Sophia Fire replied, focused.

Bootsy got the instructions that Sandy's men had unloaded everything. He said a half-hearted goodbye and left. As Bootsy was driving out of the industrial park, he called Sophia Fire for any updates.

"Sophia, talk to me. What do you see?" Bootsy was both nervous and curious now.

"The Mexicans are just leaving the industrial park. They are exiting in the opposite direction to you." As soon as Sophia Fire had said it, she noticed something unusual and said, "Hold up."

Bootsy waited a few excruciatingly long seconds for Sophia to say anything and he was about to ask before she spoke up. "The minivan is following your truck. I am getting off the roof now to assist you. Hold tight and get ready."

Bootsy's instincts were getting more right by the second. "No, do not follow me. I am going to take the long way home today; just to make sure that the minivan is following me. I need you to go home immediately and prepare for these assholes. Park your car behind the mobile home behind and make sure that your car cannot be seen from the street," he instructed.

"I understand. If anyone tries to rob us this will be their last day alive on this earth," said Sophia. She was not going to let anyone hurt Bootsy.

*****

Several hours had passed and the evening had progressed into a cloudless night. Lil Ricky and his crew had been following Bootsy for several miles along the highway, hoping for an opening. However, the men made sure to keep a safe distance from Bootsy to avoid his detection.

Lil Ricky hated waiting. He thought that catching Bootsy driving alone would have been the perfect time to rob him. Lil Ricky knew this would be the perfect opportunity to get any of the dope or some cash Bootsy was storing in his tractor trailer somewhere. It was also understood by all the men in the black minivan that they were going to have to fight or kill Bootsy to obtain his stash. However, they liked their odds of one cocky man against a few hard-ass gangbangers.

As Lil Ricky grew restless from the chase, he received a phone call from his mother.

"What's up mom, I am busy now. Can I call you back later?" He said, trying to focus as much as he could on his driving, not speeding up too much. Lil Ricky did not, however, expect his mother to start yelling.

"Hell No! You will talk to me now Ricky. Why the fuck were you at my father's restaurant?" Lisa Chin screamed at her son. "I told you for years not to fuck with him and you disobeyed me. What the fuck is your problem? Are you deaf, stupid and in need of an ass kicking? I told you I don't trust that dirty bastard."

Lil Ricky laughed. "Mom, now we both know nobody is kicking my ass. Also, when is it a crime to visit my grandfather?" He was talking cocky trying to impress his friends. Why wouldn't he? Lil Ricky was about to score big. In fact, he was in the process of accomplishing that goal now.

"Wow! Really Ricky? Do you think I'm stupid?" Lisa Chin replied. "My father does not allow anyone to visit him unless there is money involved. Now I know you did not go there for the chicken fried rice. So, what did you visit him for; was it to buy guns?" Her voice was getting more concerned than angry now.

"Mom, I am a grown ass man and the days of telling you my daily schedule are over." Lil Ricky exclaimed. His voice getting more frustrated at having to keep up with Bootsy's tractor trailer while also talking to her. "Besides, my crew and I needed some guns for protection. I can't be caught in these streets without a stick (gun)." Lil Ricky said, matter-of-factly, knowing his mother would have a thousand and one things to say about that.

"Ricky let me tell you this for the last time. Nothing never turns out good working with my father and believe me he does not give one flying fuck about you, son." Lisa said as her anger dissipated. Her voice was almost breaking as she was beginning to sob.

"Mom, you act like your hands are clean. I know about your little prescription pills operation too. You ain't slick. It is too bad that you have no more products to sell because of the big drug bust that involved your supplier. I saw that the hospital pharmacy director went to prison on RICO charges. Everyone has Unclean Hands mom. So, stop acting like you are so damn innocent. Our family will always be connected to the drugs and guns underworld. I have learned to embrace it now. You should too. I don't remember you ever being this soft," said Lil Ricky.

He continued to ignore his mother's voice and the fact that even over the phone he could imagine the tears streaking down her face. However, right now he didn't have time for sympathy. After today his mother will understand that Lil Ricky was now a man.

"Listen to yourself, son." Lisa Chin spoke, slowly, in a deep voice. She was trying to hold back tears. "That is my father's talk. Now I know you are in way over your head. Just come home and let us figure out another way you can make money legally. Doing it legally is not soft. This way you won't ever have to worry about having to have a stick (gun), or whatever you are fucking call your gun."

"It is too late for that shit mom. I don't watch things from the porch. I've jumped off the porch. I will call you later, we have some business to take care of now." Lil Ricky said as he noticed Bootsy slowing down and turning onto a rural road.

After driving for a few hours Bootsy finally arrived at his home. He owned a massive amount of land. His homestead included one single, two doublewide family mobile homes, one large storage area, a few loose dogs, chickens, and a large pig pen with ten undernourished pigs. Bootsy parked his tractor trailer next to two other vehicles located on his property. He made sure to lock his truck doors and entered his double wide mobile home. Bootsy, being a man who is always observant, knew that there were strangers following him. Therefore, he informed Sophia to prepare for a fight best she could, especially since he knew something was afoot during his latest drug delivery for Sandy Lopez drug organization.

Lil Ricky ended the phone call with his mother just as Bootsy finally reached his home. Lil Ricky and his crew parked just close enough to Bootsy house to observe his movements without being detected.

He and his crew drove closer to Bootsy's mobile home with their car's lights off. They observed Bootsy turning lights on and off inside the mobile home while he moved around in different rooms. They couldn't really tell if the man was relaxing inside or if he was scurrying about doing something.

The men waited until Bootsy to turn off all the lights inside his home before they made their move to ambush him by surprise. Lil Ricky gave the order to load their weapons and follow him. His crew put on their facemasks and approached the mobile home using stealth maneuvers they had practiced at Lil Ricky's mother's house over the last week. They didn't just want to barge in through the door but at least use some subtlety. They didn't want to damage any of the products that were stored inside.

But practicing subtlety only went so far when it came to entering Bootsy's mobile home. One couldn't really find any clear exits. Only an entrance into the mobile home was noticeable. Once Lil Ricky's crew reached the front door, they kicked it in. However, they were greeted by shotgun blasts from Bootsy. Resulting in one of Lil Ricky's crew being critically injured. The young man was launched backwards from the door to the ground, which gave the crew pause, except for Lil Ricky.

Enraged, Lil Ricky and his last remaining man charged as Bootsy was just getting up from a cover spot to shoot again before Lil Ricky lunged at him. Bootsy's shotgun was thrown onto the floor as a result. The other man came behind Lil Ricky and were able to subdue Bootsy. They started beating him with their weapons and stomping him with their feet. Bootsy fell to the floor, in a fetal position, trying to use his hands and elbows to at least dampen the blows he was receiving.

"Where the fuck is the drugs and money old man? We know you made a delivery for Sandy Lopez's organization today. Now give us the rest of the fucking drugs and all the money!" Lil Ricky exclaimed as he kicked Bootsy lying down in from of him.

Bootsy (Speaking with blood-stained teeth)

"Fuck you little nigga," Bootsy spoke. "I am not telling you shit, and you kick like a fucking fairy. Ya' twinkle toes having bitch! One of your feet feels like you are wearing a little bitch's size five shoes." He spat towards Lil Ricky and his crew, blood from his mouth flying in the air towards them like a mist, spraying the young men with it.

Lil Ricky jumped back to avoid his spit and seeing that Bootsy was not going to give any information. He told the remaining crew members to shoot Bootsy in the leg. However, before the man could complete Lil Ricky's order, Sophia Fire emerged from the back bedroom. She pointed her assault rifle at Lil Ricky's remaining crew member and shot him in the chest and head killing him instantly.

Lil Ricky's with weapon in hand was quicker to respond. He was able to get two shots off in Sophia's direction, both hitting their target. Sophia was shot in the stomach and chest by him and fell to the floor.

Amongst the chaos, Bootsy managed to retrieve his shotgun from the floor and shot Lil Ricky in his knee. Lil Ricky lay on the ground and screamed in pain as Bootsy stood to his feet. Bootsy aimed his shotgun at Lil Ricky's face and pulled the trigger. Half of Lil Ricky's head dispersed in the process, like someone had put a bomb inside his face and blown it up.

Bootsy glanced around the room, looking for any stragglers. Once he knew that things were quiet, he quickly went to Sophia' aide but it was too late. She had bled out and her body lay lifeless and still. He felt for a pulse, despite knowing he wouldn't find one and his fears were only realized more. Sophia Fire was dead. He mourned her briefly before gathering his senses. Bootsy knew exactly what to do next. He was prepared for this situation.

Bootsy wrapped all the dead bodies in blankets and started moving them from his mobile home. He dragged the bodies towards his large pig pen. Bootsy placed their clothes into a large metal barrel and set all the clothes on fire. Still sobbing over Sophia's death, he begins to cut the bodies to ensure their blood would pour out indisputably. Bootsy's hungry pigs started to squeal at the sight of the dead bodies. It had been over a month since Bootsy last fed the pigs. He threw the bodies into the pig's pen and the pigs quickly started eating gluttonously. Bootsy then walked up the dark street to find Lil Ricky's minivan with keys still in the ignition and more ammunition. He drove the car to a cleared area on his property and torched it using gasoline.

Chapter 16
Time for Some Action

Sandy Lopez's men gathered within walking distance of the FBI safe house. The men had just received their orders to kill everyone in the safe house. They were instructed to leave no witnesses alive. Sandy Lopez's men were ten strong and armed with assault rifles and C-4 explosives. However, one of the men knew that most FBI safe houses have at least one more house close by to account for potential escapes, supply runs and surveillance.

The FBI normally used two houses for witness protection operations. One house is used as the safe house and the other for an observation post to determine potential threats. Therefore, Sandy's men used a usual approach to ambush the occupants in the FBI safe house. The men surrounded the safe house and started firing their weapons. This initial attack shocked the FBI agents and AJ Black.

The chaotic symphony of gunfire echoed through the evening as Sandy Lopez's men unleashed a torrent of bullets upon the unsuspecting FBI safe houses. AJ had spent so long risking his life to protect his mother that he had forgotten what it was like to be well and truly afraid for your own life. While bullets flying overhead AJ approached one of the FBI agents.

"What the fuck is going on?" AJ Black's eyes were wide as saucers; he was petrified. "You folks assured me that this location was safe. My uncle's men are shooting at us. Please pass me a fucking gun! I must protect myself. Oh God, I knew this was a fucking bad idea." During the mayhem, AJ Black, paralyzed by fear, cursed the ill-fated decision to trust in the safety of the location.

"Get down on the fucking ground now!" yelled one of the FBI agents. However, AJ was already ducking in his fear. So much so that he hadn't realized that his head could be seen through the window. The FBI agent grabbed him by his jacket and pulled him down towards themselves. "I am calling for backup. Nobody knew you would be here with us. Unless someone spotted us in the parking lot earlier. Did you see somebody there when we left? Was it one of your uncle's guys?" The agent didn't wait for an answer. He put a few shots in the direction of the bullets.

"Shit, they're firing nonstop from every direction!" AJ glanced back to see another agent unloading bullets towards whoever this enemy was. "How long before the help arrives? We won't be able to hold off these guys for long!" said AJ Black.

"Twenty minutes tops." The FBI agent who had pulled AJ down answered. "We just need to hold them off for now. The agents in our observation house are shooting at Sandy's men too."

"Twenty fucking minutes!?" AJ Black yelled. What?! He thought to himself. How could the best subterfuge organization in the world spend 20 minutes waiting for backup in a safe house? AJ knew he could not just sit there doing nothing, hoping for these agents to get things done. He didn't want to help as much as he wanted to help himself at that moment.

"Please give me a fucking gun now!" AJ said.

The second FBI agent while still unloading onto the firing squads outside tossed him a gun, much to AJ's surprise.

"Here take this damn gun and stop fucking talking. I do not have any spare clips to give you so make your shots count. Shoot only if you need to." The agent shouted over the raining bullets.

AJ Black immediately got up and started shooting his gun towards Sandy's men. "Take this you motherfuckers and tell my uncle to eat a dick!" He shouted.

AJ saw some men run away from the safe house and he smiled. "Shit, I shot one of them, right? They are running away, hah! Bunch of pussies!" AJ said.

Both FBI agents were quiet. They knew that the men running away from the scene when they clearly had the advantage was not a good sign. Was it a trap? Unmistakably so. Where and how was the trap going to unfold? They had no idea. The best they could to was to run, stay put, or wait to be attacked again.

"Let us get out of the house through the back door. We can rendezvous with the other agents at another location." The first FBI agent said. Sensing danger as Sandy's men retreated, they decided to make a tactical retreat themselves. Unbeknownst to the FBI agents, Sandy Lopez's men had cunningly used the assault on the safe house as a diversion. They planted C-4 explosives on the gas line valve of both safe houses, setting the stage for the devastating explosion.

All the men in the house ran towards the back door of the safe house. However, just as they reached for the handle, a deafening explosion rocked the entire safe house. The force of the blast obliterated not only the safe house but also the neighboring observation house, reducing them to rubble. Even the neighboring houses were severely damaged. Nobody knew if the people living in the houses were killed in the shootout, or what happened to them. In that moment, nobody cared.

Satisfied with the chaos they had sown, Sandy's men returned to finish the job, eliminating any survivors. Oddly, the bodies of AJ Black and the FBI agents were nowhere to be found in the wreckage. However, the FBI agents that were posted in the observation house next to the safe house were all died. Sandy's men discovered AJ and the two FBI agents severely injured and hiding behind a vehicle. They wasted no time killing both AJ and the FBI agents. The men drove off just minutes before FBI backup arrived at the crime scene. One of the men called Sandy Lopez's phone.

"Jefe (Boss), it is done. No survivors or witnesses."

Sandy Lopez smiled as he sipped on some bourbon. "Excellent, now get rid of the vehicles and guns. Go straight to Mexico; you know where. I will meet you there."

Chapter 17
Trust No One

Sandy Lopez was driving on the I-10 highway the next morning heading towards Mexico. The sun was beaming down as he reached a desert area. From his vehicle he could see the horizon for miles. Clean, serene and nothing to stop him. Just how he liked it.

Some of his lower-level drug affiliates were already being arrested by the local government and the FBI. Sandy was unbothered by this news as he knew once he crossed the border that he would be untouchable by the FBI. Sandy decided to call Detective Kelly to inform him that their lucrative business partnership was now over.

"Detective Kelly, I am sure you know by now that I had to leave your city." Sandy said as soon as the call was picked up. He had a hint of pride in his voice and of relief. "I had a rat in my organization. However, we have taken care of that problem. It was a pleasure collaborating with you, my friend. Stay safe," said Sandy.

"Damn Sandy, how could you let this happen?" Detective Kelly was upset as he spoke. "I expect this type of shit from those niggers, but you Mexicans usually manage your business better than this my friend," said Detective Kelly. He knew something like this happened with drug organizations. He thought it was a long time coming anyway for Sandy Lopez's organization. Since his opportunity to exploit a certain pharmacy director had imploded. Detective Kelly knew he needed new ways to get extra revenue.

"You are so right my friend. However, our partnership is now over," informed Sandy Lopez.

"I do not like hearing that news… but I understand. You be safe in Mexico. That is where you're headed right?"

Detective Kelly asked but got no answer. The call had already been cut off.

The detective realized that his extortion and protection money schemes were quickly going to dry up. He immediately called Richard Kelly to inform him that he now had no competition in the city. Richard Kelly was now free to sell any drugs in the city but only if Detective Kelly received his protection money.

"Richard, I have some good news for you. The Mexicans were forced to leave the city. As of now, you have no competition." Detective Kelly said, proudly.

"That is great news for all of us!" Richard exclaimed. "Also, since you got rid of the Black girl selling the prescription pills, we can now sell that product to the city too. Things are starting to look up here. Stop by the car dealership later. I want to reward you with a brand-new car of your choice."

Detective Kelly got excited at the news. "That is great! I will call you soon to pick up that vehicle and some cash if you don't mind. I'm running a little low and could also use some gas money!"

*****

Later that day, Sandy Lopez reached the Mexico border and easily crossed the checkpoint. He always had the papers and the passports needed for when things like this happened. Sandy knew that this wouldn't go well with the bosses. However, he didn't know how much they knew already about destroying the FBI safehouse where his nephew had been stashed. Sandy went to his retreat; only to find a reckoning waiting for him. When he arrived at his village Sandy was not greeted with a warm welcome. The drug cartel that he worked for was terribly upset that Sandy allowed a million dollar a month operation to be destroyed by his nephew AJ Black. As

Sandy walked into his plush estate to find his beloved sister Maria gagged and tied to a chair.

Sandy Lopez's face was frozen in shock and fear. He never expected things to be this bad. "Wait, what are you doing? Everything is okay. I bought you all the money owed to you and the drugs. We left no witnesses. So, we are free to sell our product in a new location!" Sandy began explaining himself, but he was shut down by the boss.

"Sandy Lopez," said a large man with a hoarse tone. The man wearing a very sharp suit that seemed more expensive than the estate. "The money…" he said, pointing towards a stack of cash near Maria.

"….and drugs…" He said, pointing towards the dope next to his sister on the other side. "…is not the problem. You allowed that fucking nephew that you vouch for to fuck up our operation. That is a million dollars per month that we cannot get back. You must look at the big picture."

Sandy Lopez began to cry. "Please do not do this to us." He went down to his knees, tears streaming down his face. "I can be a high earner for you again. Just let me show you. Please don't do this to us. Let me show you." Sandy said as he palmed his hands together, almost like in prayer.

"My friend, it is way too late to do that now." The boss walked towards Sandy and touched his face, in pity. "I love you and your sister. I do dearly. However, you know the consequences and now you and your sister must pay the price."

The cartel boss ordered his men to behead both Sandy Lopez and his sister.

Without hesitation a small sweaty man with long wavy hair came from the left side of the room with a machete in hand, serving two swift waving movements. As was custom for betrayal; both heads were placed on wooden stakes at the entrance of Sandy Lopez's Mexico estate for all to see. The cartel boss left their heads there as a warning to all in the area.

He would not tolerate any fuck ups, no excuses.

Chapter 18

Untrustworthy

Things were always a little rocky between the Detective Kelly and the car dealership owner, Richard Kelly. Despite their lucrative partnership, the detective was always wary of Richard and his decidedly selfish and brash antics. Then again, Richard Kelly himself always knew that the superficial dirty police officer would do about anything for money.

The news of some of Sandy Lopez's crew being arrested, and Sandy himself having to flee the city spread like wildfire. In the chaos, some people wanted to lay their claim on the territory of Sandy Lopez, while others simply wanted to use this opportunity to get out of the game finally. Some citizens of the city were now experiencing emotions of fear and horror, while others felt glinting at the promise of new opportunities.

For Richard, however, this was something else, as it opened the door to untold wealth.

The previous evening, Richard Kelly was made aware of some news that shocked him about his go-to person Detective Kelly. Richard was shocked to discover that the detective was also working with his main drug competitor Sandy Lopez. Although at first, he did want to believe the news. However, the detective had informed him that he was now the only major drug supplier in the city. Richard's informant information was proven to be correct that Detective Kelly was working with not one but two of his drug organization's rivalries. He now knew that Detective Kelly couldn't be trusted.

Richard Kelly had years of experience dealing with underworld figures and despite his brashness he knew how to use subterfuge and the art of below-the-belt actions better than most. He was a man who had spies in places one wouldn't believe. His network of paid informants helped ensure his longevity in the illegal drug business. His entire network was decentralized. No spy knew about the existence of any other. He had ten different people verifying everything and none of the ten knew about anyone else. Richard had watched empires rise and fall. Yet he would remain like a voyeuristic force of nature, of sorts.

Detective Kelly himself was unaware of the car dealership owner informants were watching his every move. The detective was not the only dirty police officer in the city. Others had noticed the detective's unknown source of wealth and wanted to acquire some riches for themselves too. Richard Kelly was a smart businessperson and believed in checks and balances. He made sure that he had leverage when he needed it. However, he never made others aware of his intentions. Richard would even use extorting tactics if it would help him sell his drugs.

The thought of Detective Kelly's betrayal made Richard more upset because he believed he could be trusted. Repeatedly he had chosen not to believe some questionable things about the detective. However, traitors had no place in Richard Kelly's organization. The detective was now a wild card and Richard quickly thought of a plan to dispose of him. He would tell Detective Kelly to meet him at a new location to pick up the vehicle he promised earlier.

Richard Kelly called up the detective. He was going to take the wild card out of the game. "Detective Kelly!" He said, joyfully. "I have a change of plan regarding your new car. We are having brand new cars delivered to my new car dealership and as a token of my appreciation, I want you to have your pick of any car you wish directly off the trailer! I wanted you to be the one to pop the cherry of this new dealership, hah!" laughed Richard.

Detective Kelly wasn't too quick to respond. The past few days had been chaotic to say the least, from the murders to the burning people and the organizations that had seen their rise and collapse. Therefore, he noticed that Richard's offer being out of the man's character and could be a setup.

"Sure, I will meet you at the new dealership." Detective Kelly said, trying his best to sound enthused, but being incredibly suspicious. The detective had recently lost some potentially lucrative opportunities because they were too dangerous to keep. The city's illegal drugs business was in a transition period and power was changing hands. It wasn't a suitable time to be rewarded this soon and highly unusual he thought. "Please provide me with the address and time. Also, thank you again for the generous gift" said Detective Kelly.

"Not a problem, detective." Richard replied. "I will text you the address and the cars will be delivered at 9pm tonight. Just pick the car and my staff will give you the title and keys.

Thanks again for what you've done for my business." Both men ended their phone conversation.

Richard Kelly called his other go-to person, the enforcer Sal Antonio, with instructions on how to dispose of Detective Kelly. He knew by killing a police officer it would only be a matter of time before the police and federal government would be investigating Detective Kelly's murder. However, he had a contiguous plan for a situation like this one. Richard had already purchased a beautiful villa in Costa Rica. That country had tight extradition laws. He also established offshore accounts years ago and had taken several solo trips to his property over the years.

It was time to clean the house. He had lost a trusted friend and made an enemy while conducting business in this city. Richard decided it was time to turn the page and retire among sunny beaches and beautiful villas in a location where there was eternal summer.

He called up his go-to person, who picked up at the first ring.

"Sal, we have a problem. You know that the detective has been playing both sides of the fence with us, right? That pig has been working for our competitors and us long enough. His actions cannot go unpunished. I need you to take care of this problem for me tonight."

Sal Antonio smirked at the thought of finally getting rid of the police officer. "I never trusted that fucking pig. How would you like me to manage it, boss?"

"I believe you should take care of him the same way you did Alcia Adams. Just make sure his body is not on our property when it is discovered." Richard replied.

"It would be my pleasure to kill this disloyal man for you. It will be done as you instructed." Sal Antonio put down the phone and began to prepare for his mission.

*****

Hours later after the call, Detective Kelly had a feeling that something was not right with this new meeting change of location. The fact that Richard Kelly was giving him something on a silver platter for nothing was puzzling. If anything, it was time for him to lay low. It was just something in Richard Kelly's voice that had him uneased. The detective had been playing both sides so he could always come out on top. However, he now realized that the only way one would ever win this dirty game was to be the one that made the rules. This time, it was clear that he was in way over his head. Detective Kelly decided to enlist some help, making sure that the help was as uninformed as it needed to be. So, Detective Kelly decided to send police officer Cynthia Brown in his place.

"Officer Brown, I have a favor to ask you," said Detective Kelly. "I was supposed to meet my informant tonight. He is going to provide information on a new shipment of drugs coming to the city. However, I have prior commitments and they changed the location of the meeting. Can you meet with the informant for me?"

Cynthia, being the ever-optimistic police officer, could never have refused such a request and the detective knew that. "Sure detective. Just give me the location and time. Should I have a backup police officer to assist me?" asked police officer Brown.

"No. This should be just a routine gathering of information. However, if something doesn't feel right with you when you arrive, simply, leave the location and call me" informed the detective.

Cynthia Brown was a bit concerned about that last comment. However, she brushed it off as a regular precaution. It was risky, both for the police officer and the informant, to meet each other…anywhere she thought. Of course, suspicion would invite skepticism and caution; this was more cautionary than the former.

"Will do sir and thank you for allowing me to assist you in this case," she said and packed her things before getting up to leave.

*****

Cynthia Brown arrived at the meeting location under the cover of the cloudy night sky. It was at Richard Kelly's new car dealership that was still under construction. She parked her undercover police car and walked towards the back entrance of the car dealership. Much of the dealership construction was completed. However, there were still some areas under heavy construction. The only lights working in the facility were inside the showroom. Cynthia noticed a man walking towards her and at first, thought he was her contact. She was in her plain clothes with her badge and gun were well hidden. Therefore, she had no fear for her safety while meeting the informant.

"Hello?" She called out, but the man didn't stop, or even respond. He was gaining on her, getting closer and closer and with each step, Cynthia grew nervous.

Sensing that something was not right, she immediately pulled her weapon thinking that this might be an ambush. However, before she could determine the danger of this situation, the unknown man started firing his weapon at her.

She was hit with bullets in her chest, leg, and arm as she ran for cover. Cynthia was grateful she was wearing a bulletproof vest that evening. She had prepared herself prior to this meeting because the detective's comment about the potential of this meeting turning in the wrong direction had bugged her. Although the vest had protected her vital organs, her leg and arm were still wounded.

She moved as fast as she could to avoid the bullets. Cythina was holding her good hand over the wound on her arm and trying her best to keep weight off the injured leg. She managed to hide in an office. However, Cynthia was leaving a blood trail for the man to follow. She was trying her best to stifle her screams while hiding. She managed to hide in a corner of an office and pulled out her weapon.

The man confidently walked in the office where she was hiding, trying to get in close to kill her with one shot. However, before he could complete the assassination, Cynthia aimed her weapon at the man and pulled the trigger.

She shot the man in the stomach. The unknown man then dropped his gun and screamed in pain. He dropped to the floor with a loud thud. Cynthia tried to get in close as best she could with her vision fading for the kill shot. She got close enough to finally see the man's face. He was unfamiliar to her at first. The man started cussing at her in what seemed like Italian.

"Pezzo di Merda (Piece of Shit) (P!" He screamed. "Cazzo infiere (Fucking hell)!" Cynthia Brown managed to get to her feet and aim her gun at the man. However, before she could pull the trigger the man yelled. "Fottiti (Fuck you), you were not supposed to be here!" She recognized him, even with her fading vision. Bang.

Cythina Brown shot the man at close range. It was someone who worked for Richard Kelly's car dealership. This man was connected to Richard Kelly Ford and Nissan.

Chapter 19
Plan "B"

"Where is the bacon honey?" Richard Kelly barked, waiting at the breakfast table in his house. He had been expecting some good news by the time he woke up but hadn't gotten any messages from Sal Antonio yet. Richard wasn't too worried. Sal always preferred to do things in person. That was another reason Richard liked keeping him around. However, today was different; with every passing minute, Richard was getting uneasy.

"Coming." Richard Kelly's wife came from the kitchen, wearing an apron and holding a plate full of bacon and sausages. "It'll just be a minute," she said.

"You always say a minute and take ten. What's with you woman? I want my breakfast." Richard's patience was wearing thin. His mind was too preoccupied with waiting for Sal to think about what he was going to eat anymore. As if on its own, his hand began moving and he grabbed a large piece of bacon with his fork and ate it whole.

There was so much at stake and so much in motion, he thought. It was the perfect time to escape. The detective would have been dead by now and the open window to escape this blasted city was now. Richard knew that he could never have kept the ruse going for much longer, no matter how many cars were sold.

Mrs. Kelly was still busy in the kitchen and Richard was getting even more uneasy. The sound of the kitchen utensils banging against the plates, of his wife cutting…something, everything was getting to him. To drown it out, he decided to turn on the TV and switch on the channel to the news, hoping to catch a story about a murdered body being found or something. It was still early, but not too early. Soon, his name was heard on TV and just as it did, his wife came with a few sandwiches on a plate. Sitting down, the TV blared.

And here, there were certainly some shocking scenes at the site of the new Richard Kelly Nissan dealership under construction this morning. The construction crew found a body that had been brutally shot…

'Ah,' Richard thought. Sal hadn't managed to remove the body from his new dealership location. Richard was visibly upset as he thought of this situation. It was unusual for Sal Antonio to take a risk like this especially when Richard's name was attached to that risk. But all thought of that escaped him with what he heard next.

The police officer involved in the scene was rushed to the ER and has been confirmed to have been wounded by the assailant. It was also confirmed that the lifeless body was one Sal Antonio, who is believed to be an employee of that dealership. It is still unclear whether this has anything to do with the dealership itself, the officers on scene have so far refused to comment, pending an investigation. We have the statement of one Detective Kelly, who is the lead investigator of this case.

Both Mr. and Mrs. Kelly stopped eating. The news reported of Sal Antonio's death and that the officer being injured was shocking to both.

"Richard, did you know anything about this?" Mrs. Kelly asked. Richard remained quiet.

"Wait, isn't that Sal? Our Sal? Sal Antonio? Oh my god! Isn't he the one that you had mentored as a teen?" his wife exclaimed, pointing at the TV with a fork but Richard remained quiet.

"Richard, can you hear me? Did you know about this? Is Sal involved with something? I hope he isn't. All those years getting him on his feet. I hope he hadn't thrown it all away for a quick buck."

"What the hell?" Richard finally spoke. "I…I cannot believe this happened." He wiped his face with a napkin, still thinking. "Poor Sal."

He looked towards his wife. "I am going to the car dealership right away." He got up as he said it. "The location was still under construction, and no one should have been able to access the facility except for the construction crew" informed Richard Kelly.

Mrs. Kelly got up with him. "Yes dear, please keep me informed of the details. I hope Sal was not doing anything illegal. Let me know whatever happens. Hope the young man wasn't involved in anything illegal."

Richard Kelly turned around towards his wife just as he had begun to go towards the door. "Dear, all I can do is lead them type of people to the water. I cannot make them drink the damn thing. It is going to be a long day at work. Do not expect a call from me until later tonight." he said, grabbing his keys and wallet from the table.

"Okay baby. Still, keep me posted. Text me if you find out anything. I will only call you if it is an emergency." Mrs. Kelly went forward towards Richard.

Richard Kelly kissed his wife goodbye and grabbed his coat in a half-sprint towards the car. He almost did a burnout and skidded the car through a few turns as he drove towards the car dealership. His wife had followed Richard outside and was watching him drive away.

After a few turns he was finally out of sight from his wife's point of view. Right after that, Richard turned his car in the direction of the highway leading out of the city. He stopped at a gas station near the highway exit to refuel his car and pick up snacks for a long journey. It was time to put his plan B in operation.

*****

Richard Kelly had been driving for over five hours on I-95 South when his cell phone buzzed. He picked it up and saw that it was his wife calling. He could do nothing other than to leave it ringing. He pressed the volume button to silence the noise and ignored her call.

On the ride he saw cars passing by him. Some were new, the kind you'd see in commercials rather than car lots. He thought of the cars he would sell. Bling over everything else for some and bang over buck for others. He had made a fortune by making people give too much for too little and he wasn't about to let that fortune go.

It was high time that he carved out a piece of the world for himself and lived his life in peace. Richard Kelly was getting older and tired. However, he thought about the people driving pass him in their cars, singles, couples, and families. He reminisced about how he had cheated many like them and how easy it was to convinced them to pay high interest loans on cars they really couldn't afford. However, before his thoughts could continue it was replaced with the annoying sound of his cell phone once again.

Richard pressed the volume button again to quiet it down, and continued to drive towards Miami, Florida. Two hours later, his wife called again and left him a message. He guessed it might be a long one, because she would have a lot to say to him. An hour later, his wife again, but this time, the calls persisted. His wife was refusing to leave a message, too. She was determined to talk to him directly.

Once Richard Kelly arrived in Miami-Dade County, Florida, he purchased a cheap prepaid cell phone from Walmart. He paid for six months of cell phone services in advance and drove towards the White Point Boat Marina. Richard wasn't here for a vacation. At the marina, Richard had chartered a small boat to take him to the Bahamas. Once he felt safe there, then he would listen to his wife's phone messages. Right now, his trail was too fresh. By now, the word was surely out that a certain owner of a dealership had just seemingly left town when an employee of his had been shot by the police the previous night.

Richard arrived in Nassau in the Bahamas and rapidly purchased a one-way plane ticket to Costa Rica. Since he had a couple of hours before his plane departed, Richard decided to grab something to eat. He had time to kill. He ordered some lobster and baked crab. Richard wasn't going to skimp on his last meal while on the run.

Once he finished his meal, Richard decided to listen to his wife's phone messages. It was high time that he let the past go. However, before washing away the little slivers of guilt he still had, Richard picked up his phone and played the first of many messages that he saw on screen.

Richard honey, please call me back. There are some gentlemen here from the police department wanting to talk to you about Sal Antonio. They went to your office to talk to you, but you were out of the office at that time, honey. I told them you went to lunch or left to assist Sal's family with his funeral arrangements. The gentlemen are asking about your whereabouts, and I don't really know if you're somewhere on business or out for lunch. Call me back baby and let me know, love you.

The phone went silent. A glint of a tear appeared on Richard Kelly's face. However, he quickly wiped it away before he played the next one.

Richard, what is going on? Where are you? The FBI is now at our house and the news media is here too. Even our neighbors are outside our house. I am scared. They are tearing our house apart looking for documents. They are not telling me what you did or what Sal did or what anyone else is involved in. Richard, what did you do? What is going on Richard? Please call me back.

A smile appeared on Richard's face. He knew they would waste hours, if not days, skimming through and searching in places where there was no substance. The only thing they would find are the documents that any citizen would have and if they had broken into the office of his dealership by now, they'd find the same documents submitted to the IRS, forged or otherwise.

Richard went on to the next message and pressed play.

Damn you, Richard! The FBI has shown me photos of you and another woman with a little boy. They are looking for drugs in our home. Where the fuck are you? The Social Services department has taken our children. Whatever you have done please come back and make this right. The FBI is talking about arresting me on conspiracy charges. Why is this happening? Who are those people? Who is that woman? Call me right fucking now!

There was just one message after this and then nothing. Richard took a deep breath and pressed play on the final message.

You son of a bitch! You had me sign all those fucking business documents when we first got married and I never read any of them. You put all the companies in my damn name! The FBI is going to send me to prison. I am the mother of your two sons. I deserve better treatment from you. So do our kids. I hope you rot in hell for this Richard Fucking Kelly!! You fat dirty ass white bellied asshole! Rot in hell you evil piece of shit. Fuck you.

Richard Kelly laughed after hearing his wife's phone messages. Every cuss and scream were like music to his ears. The only way they could ever make him appear was if he could be a witness against his own wife, who'd been the 'real brains' of the operation. He'd make a deal in a few years, where he could testify against her and get any charges against him dropped. He was 'duped' by a much more sinister and cleverer woman, wasn't he? 'Blinded by love,' he'd say in court.

Laughing, he then tossed his old cell phone in the trash as he boarded his plane. He was flying in first class, a direct flight. Richard was pleased as the plane reached flying altitude. He knew the US government could not touch him in Costa Rica. Even if they tried, his record was clean there.

When Richard arrived in Costa Rica, he was greeted by a beautiful young woman and a little boy named Richard. The boy was named after his father. Richard Sr. hugged and kissed them both and they were driven by a driver towards his marbled villa in a brand-new Nissan.

*****

Cynthia Brown was in stable condition at the local hospital back in town. To ensure her safety, the police department had a guard posted outside her room until the location of Richard Kelly was acknowledged. Richard Kelly was a person of great interest to the local authorities and the FBI, though they were still undecided on whether it was Richard or his wife that were truly the right people to consider as suspects—or even both.

Many had already begun speculating that anyone thinking it was Mrs. Kelly that ran the show would be delusional at best, and stupid at worst. Nobody could ever doubt that a man like Richard Kelly (already a known scammer because of his dealership) could easily run a crime ring; especially one that dealt in hardcore drugs.

The police were out in full force that morning; with calls left and right about captures, potential witnesses, suspects and much more.

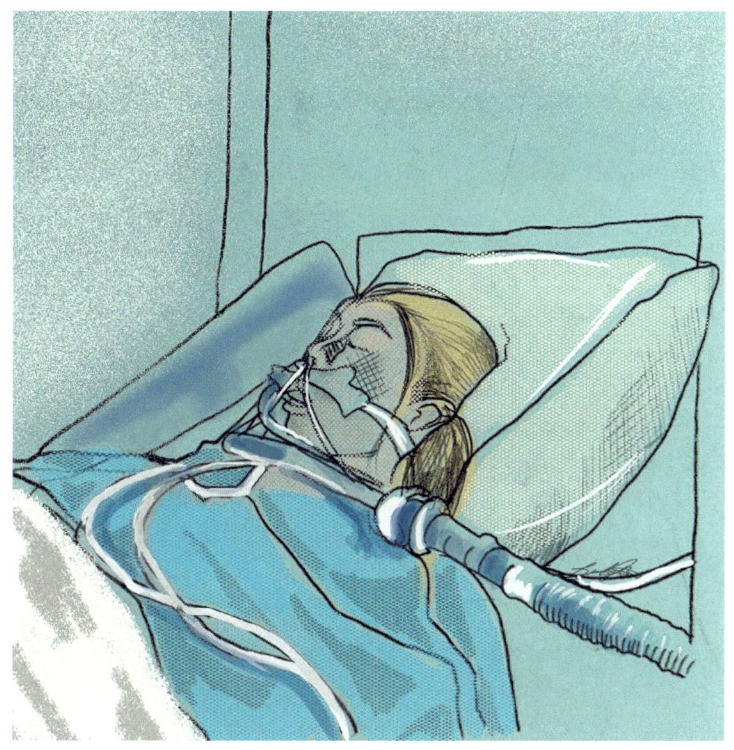

As she lay in the hospital bed, Cynthia Brown contemplated her entire ordeal. She concluded that Detective Kelly set her up to be ambushed, but why? Cynthia posed no threat to him, yet he wanted her dead. She half considered that it might have been the detective that would be the one being set up in the first place. However, she imagined that too be too much of a coincidence.

Just as her blood started to boil from her anger, Detective Kelly entered her room, surprising the police officer. Detective Kelly looked at Cynthia with a smile. "Officer Brown, how are you feeling? I am so sorry for what happened to you. You gave us all a scare earlier. We did not know if you were going to pull through your surgery. Thank God you are still with us. I've been praying for you!"

The officer stationed outside was still there and Cynthia eyed him to reassure her of protection. However, before Cynthia Brown could respond to the detective, he leaned over her bed and talked in her ear.

"Look, at this moment I can kill you and no one can help you." Detective Kelly said in a menacing voice, enough to make Cynthia freeze. "Matter of fact, I can kill you anytime I want to and there is nothing no one can do to prevent this from happening. Now you can either die here today or work for me. The choice is yours and you will only have this opportunity to answer me once."

Detective Kelly backed up and flashed his smile once again. He was staring at a white-faced Cynthia, who looked like all her blood had drained from her face.

"Cheer up. You already made it through the rough part. It's all in the job description of being a good police officer. Moments like these happen. It is not that bad. This is how you earn your stripes. I promise you when I get promoted you will get promoted too. We both will raise up the ranks fast. I need you to be my eyes and ears in this city. (In a more serious tone) You will pick up the money and I will be the enforcer. One day I am going to be Police Chief and you will be my second in command."

Police officer Cynthia Brown knowing she had no choice and with tears running down her face answered him. "I accepted your offer, detective. I will work for you." Cynthia said, tears streaming down her face.

*****

Mr. Chin parked his car in the alley behind his restaurant, the Chinese Express, the next morning.

He was whistling as he got out of his car and straightened his coat. He looked around, still whistling, and breathed. There will be some new people coming into town soon, buyers looking for a new supplier for guns. They needed someone reliable, someone like him, a partner. However, Mr. Chin always thoroughly investigated his buyers before any transactions. He never did a business deal without stacking all the cards in his favor.

As Mr. Chin neared his restaurant rear entrance, he did a quick observation of his surroundings again. However, he didn't really notice a figure silently approaching him as he reached the door at his restaurant. Mr. Chin reached into his pocket, took out his keys and unlocked the back door. He had just opened the door, not even having stepped in yet, when there was a loud bang.

Mr. Chin stopped in his tracks. At first, it was the sound that had startled him. However, he didn't move. Mr. Chin couldn't move. He felt something…something wet, drip down his shirt. Mr. Chin put his hand there and felt it. Moist, sticky, but very, very apparent as to what it was. Even before his eyes saw it, he knew.

Blood.

Someone had walked up behind him and shot him in the back.

Mr. Chin managed to turn his head towards the shooter standing right behind him as he fell to the ground. His vision was still clear, even at his age. He saw his daughter Lisa Chin standing over him.

Mr. Chin managed to whisper out to ask her a last question. "Why Lisa, my daughter? I thought we were a family again."

Lisa Chin spat in his face and immediately started firing her handgun until there were no bullets left.

Bang. Bang. Bang.

Bang. Bang. Bang.

It was not until the gun had stopped smoking that Lisa finally answered her father's question, with tears in her eyes and a broken voice.

"That was for my son and his father. Now I will run this shit from this point moving forward, dad."

Lisa Chin drove her away from the restaurant with tears in her eyes as she finally realized her son was right. In this city, everyone has Unclean Hands.

About the Author

Aubrey Boyd has written screenplays and novels in the genres of drama, comedy, horror, kids, and conspiracy theories. With the help of family and friends he will continue to be inspired to share stories with interesting characters and moral messages.

Aubrey holds degrees in aeronautical engineering, general studies, emergency disaster management and a master's degree in emergency management. He served in the US Navy and received an honorable discharge. He has traveled the world and lived-in unique locations that have allowed him to create intriguing stories. He adores and enjoys the company of his family and friends.

Made in the USA
Columbia, SC
17 February 2025

53976709R00165